The ʼʼʼ

**AND HEROES
COLLECTION**

The Playboys and Heroes large print collection
gives you lavish stories of luxury
from your favourite top authors
in easier-to-read print.

ROYAL AFFAIRS: THE ROYAL WEDDING NIGHT

Day Leclaire

First published in Great Britain 2008
by Mills & Boon, an imprint of Harlequin (UK) Limited,
Large Print edition 2012
Harlequin (UK) Limited,
Eton House, 18-24 Paradise Road, Richmond, Surrey TW9 1SR

© Day Totton Smith 2007

ISBN: 978 0 263 23053 6

11795378

Harlequin (UK) policy is to use papers that are natural, renewable and recyclable products and made from wood grown in sustainable forests. The logging and manufacturing process conform to the legal environmental regulations of the country of origin.

Printed and bound in Great Britain
by CPI Antony Rowe, Chippenham, Wiltshire

Day Leclaire is the multi-award-winning author of nearly forty novels. Her passionate books offer a unique combination of humour, emotion and unforgettable characters, which have won Day tremendous worldwide popularity, as well as numerous publishing honours. She is a threetime winner of both a Colorado Award of Excellence and a Golden Quill Award. She's won a *RT Book Reviews* Career Achievement Award and a Love and Laughter Award, a Holt Medallion, a Booksellers Best Award, and she has received an impressive ten nominations for the prestigious Romance Writers of America RITA® Award. Day's romances touch the heart and make you care about her characters as much as she does. In Day's own words, "I adore writing romances and can't think of a better way to spend each day."

CHAPTER ONE

Principality of Avernos, Verdonia—
How it all began...

"No. No way, no how. You're not doing this, Miri. I don't care what you say or do. I won't have you involved in any of this."

She threw off her cover-up to reveal the wedding gown she wore beneath. She didn't care how much he loomed over her, she wasn't about to back down. Her other royal stepbrother, Lander, had long been dubbed the "Lion of Mt. Roche." But Merrick reminded her more of a golden leopard than the king of beasts. Maybe that had something to do with his being whipcord lean and sleek, and deadly silent until he moved in for an attack. Not to mention possessing a speed and agility she'd never seen bested.

"It's too late, Merrick. I'm already involved."

His mouth compressed at the sight of her gown, and he pinned her with a merciless gaze. "Only because you listened in on a private conversation." He nodded knowingly. "Yes, you damn well should blush. Hell, Miri. I'm the head of Verdonia's Royal Security Force. If I'd caught anyone else doing what you did, I'd have thrown them in the deepest, darkest pit I could find. Worse, if anyone in a position of authority had found out you'd spied, I'd have been forced to act. My own sister!"

"You need my help," she insisted stubbornly.

He gripped her shoulders and gave her a gentle shake. "Listen to me, honey, this is serious. Abducting a woman…it could mean jail for everyone involved."

"Then it means jail." She shot Merrick a stony glare, utilizing every ounce of logic she could summon—a difficult proposition when raw emotion held her in its grip. "Think about it. You're planning to abduct Princess Alyssa minutes before her wedding. Don't you think the groom's going to notice when his bride goes missing? You need someone to take her place at the altar. To fool people just long enough so you have time to get away."

He thrust a hand through hair streaked every color from blond to umber. "The operative words here are 'get away.' I get away. My men get away. Even Alyssa gets away, if not by choice. You're the one left at von Folke's mercy. What do you think will happen when he unveils you—literally—and discovers you're not Princess Alyssa Sutherland, political ally. Instead, he's married Princess Miri Montgomery, sister of his political foe. Or have you forgotten that von Folke and Lander are rivals for the throne of Verdonia?"

She dismissed the question with a sweep of her hand. "Of course I haven't forgotten. But do you really think Prince Brandt will have me arrested? Throw me into prison? How will that look five short months before the election to choose our next king?"

"Von Folke isn't going to be happy," Merrick replied, before adding beneath his breath, "and that has to be the understatement of the year. There's no question in my mind that he'll take out his unhappiness on someone. I don't want that someone to be you."

"Brandt wouldn't hurt me. At least…not the way you mean."

"You can't be certain of that." Merrick started hammering away again. "He might find another way to get even for the theft of his bride. I won't allow him to use you for that purpose. Not when I'm the one responsible."

"Nor will I." She stood in a copy of another woman's wedding gown, trembling from a combination of fury and heartbreak. "I have it all planned out. When it's time for the unveiling at the end of the ceremony, I'm going to refuse to allow it. I'll fake an illness, if I have to. I'll ask them to take me to my room—Alyssa's room—until I can recover. And the instant I'm alone, I'll change into whatever of hers fits and leave."

"Just like that? You don't think anyone will stop you?" Merrick folded his arms across his chest. "You can't be that naive."

Miri lifted an eyebrow. "Why would anyone stop me? After all, I'm just a guest at the wedding, not the bride. It'll be Miri Montgomery who strolls out the front door, not Princess Alyssa Sutherland von Folke. Now, stop arguing, Merrick. If you don't like my idea, then work on perfecting the plan. What can we change so it will work?"

"There's no point in perfecting or changing anything. I won't allow you to go through with this."

"You'll do it." She played her final card. "You'll do it, or I'll tell big brother what you're planning."

She may have pushed him too far. Anger sent

twin flags of color flaring across his cheek-bones. "You'd involve Lander?"

"In a heartbeat."

"If you tell him, if you involve him in this, he'll lose any chance at the throne. He'll be an accessory."

She grasped Merrick's hands in hers. "Then let me help you. If your plan succeeds, Lander will sit on the throne. Isn't that what you want?"

"That's not why I'm doing this," he instantly denied. "All I want is a fair election. That won't happen if von Folke marries Princess Alyssa. If he gains her as a political ally, the throne is as good as his."

"Fine. We're both doing it for the good of Verdonia. I just want your plan to succeed and I'm the best person to make sure that happens. Now, are we through here?" She gestured toward the door. "Do we go switch brides now, or do you want to waste more time arguing?"

Sheer stubbornness turned his eyes a molten

gold and for a full thirty seconds she was certain she'd lost. Then he gave an abrupt nod and Miri allowed her breath to escape in a silent sigh of relief. She turned toward the door, but he stopped her before she could open it.

"Not so fast." Drawing her deeper into the room of the cottage he'd rented, he examined her appearance with a critical eye. "What the hell did you do to your hair?"

She touched the loose curls self-consciously. "Your man said Alyssa was a blonde. I figured my disguise would hold up a little better if I bleached it."

"Can you turn it back...after?"

She actually managed to smile at the hint of alarm in his voice. "Yes, I can turn it back. You like it dark better than blond?"

"On you, yes."

How ironic. From the day her mother had married Merrick's father, King Stefan, she'd wanted to look like the rest of the Montgomerys, all of whom were tall and athletic and striking, their streaked hair and hazel eyes kissed with golden sunshine. Her coal-black hair and pale green eyes had always made her feel like an outsider, as did the fact that she was a princess by adoption and proclamation, rather than birth. Only with Brandt had she ever felt—

To her relief, Merrick broke in before she could complete the thought. "It just might work," he conceded reluctantly. "From the photos I've seen, you're close in height and body shape."

"That was my biggest concern."

"It's not mine," he retorted, a sharp edge to his words. "When it's time for you to leave as Miri Montgomery, people might wonder why you've bleached your hair blond, especially when they see you exiting Alyssa's room."

"You think it'll rouse suspicion?" She shook her head. "They'll think I've made a poor fashion choice, that's all. It won't occur to them it's because I took the bride's place at the altar.

As for being in Alyssa's room…I was helping the bride, poor dear. Something she ate didn't agree with her, I suspect. She's asked that no one disturb her for a bit. Just give her an hour or two to rest and she'll be fine. Oh, and perhaps you'd deliver a message to Prince Brandt? Tell him that his bride is looking forward to joining him a little later this evening, after she's had some private time to recover."

Merrick looked far from happy. "It might work."

"It *will* work."

"Don't get cocky, Miri. You're not a perfect match. And it's far from a perfect plan."

"So, I'll improvise. With luck no one will notice the discrepancies, especially not beneath a veil. You'll need to give me Alyssa's. If I wear a different veil…that is something women will notice."

"I'll make sure you have it." His voice turned gruff. "You look—You look incredible, sweetheart. I just wish this were real, that you were standing here dressed for your own wedding, instead of for this farce."

His words struck like a blow, though he couldn't possibly have known. She forced out a careless smile and prayed her voice would hold steady. "Thank you. But I'd need a fiancé for that, wouldn't I?" Too bad the man she'd had in mind was no longer interested, despite what he'd once claimed.

An odd expression drifted across Merrick's face, one she could have only described as "brotherly." Tucking a strand of hair behind her ear, he shrugged. "You're only twenty-five. There's plenty of time to fall in love." He made a production of checking his watch, then gestured toward the door. "Time to go. We're cutting this close as it is."

Miri preceded her brother from the cottage he'd rented as a command center and allowed him to help her into the passenger seat of a silver-gray SUV. Behind them his men piled into a matching black one, which tailed them at a circumspect speed through the hilly roads of Verdonia's northernmost principality of Avernos. Nerves prevented her from attempting idle chatter, not that she'd have had any opportunity. Merrick spent the entire trip filling her in on every detail he'd uncovered about Princess Alyssa, no matter how minor. Half an hour passed before the two cars turned down a narrow country road. Less than a mile farther along they veered onto a dirt shoulder.

Leaving the car to idle, Merrick swiveled in his seat to look at her. "Listen to me, Miri. This shouldn't take long. No more than twenty minutes." He tapped the car clock. "If we're not back in that time precisely, you are to get behind the wheel and drive away. Head straight south from Avernos all the way through Celestia until you reach Verdon, and don't stop until you get there. Don't come looking for me. Don't call anyone. Just get the hell out. Are we clear?"

"Clear."

He shook his head. "I'm serious, Miri. I want your word of honor. If I don't return in twenty minutes, swear to me you'll leave without intervening in any way."

They were the two most difficult words she'd ever spoken. "I swear."

He nodded in satisfaction. Climbing out of the SUV, he signaled to his men. The four of them, all dressed in melt-into-the-shadows black, slid ominous hoods over their heads as they trotted across the expanse of grass beside the road and headed toward a small ridge half hidden by a dense expanse of deciduous forest. Miri inched forward in her seat and kept her gaze glued on the car clock. The seconds crept by, one by one, until after an hour—or what seemed like an hour—a mere fifteen minutes had piled up onto the clock.

At nineteen minutes, thirty seconds, Merrick emerged from the woods. He held a woman in his arms, a woman wearing a silver gown that proved a close match to Miri's. A flowing lace

and tulle veil sat askew on her long blond curls.
Princess Alyssa Sutherland. She was absolutely
stunning, Miri noted with a sinking heart. And
a bit shorter than she, herself, was. But that
shouldn't present a problem. She'd brought an
extra pair of shoes to cover just that eventual-
ity. Switching the ones she wore for the pair
with the lowest heels, she opened the car door
and headed toward Merrick.

"It's time," he said, as she approached. "You
don't have to go through with this. You can
still change your mind."

"I can't and I won't. There are…reasons."

She didn't dare explain further. If Merrick
knew the truth, he'd never have agreed to involve her. At the sound of her voice, Princess
Alyssa stiffened. She started to turn her head
to look, but his grip tightened, preventing her.

"Quickly, Merrick," Miri warned. "We have
only moments until her disappearance is discovered."

Ripping the voluminous veil from Alyssa's head, he tossed it to Miri. "Will this work?"

"It's perfect. From what I can tell our dresses are nearly identical. The veil will definitely conceal any discrepancies." She shot a wary glance toward Princess Alyssa and switched from English to Verdonian. From what Merrick had said, the woman had been raised in the United States and, until she'd flown out to marry Brandt, hadn't been in Verdonia since she was a toddler. Chances were excellent she didn't speak the language.

"Be careful with this one," she warned, nodding toward the woman Merrick held. "I know how you are around beautiful women. She's liable to turn you from a grizzly to a teddy bear."

Merrick gave a short, gruff laugh. "Don't worry about me. Worry about yourself," he said in a surprisingly tender voice. "Compared to von Folke, I really am a teddy bear. Go now. Head straight through the woods. There's a chapel about a hundred yards in. You'll find a guard unconscious in the garden just beyond the chapel walls. Put on your veil and sit next to him. When he comes to, tell him he passed out. Tell him whatever you think will work, but don't let him report the incident."

She nodded in understanding. Without another word, she hurried into the woods, picking her way as swiftly as possible through the underbrush, careful to make certain that the layers of skirting didn't snag on any of the shrubs. If she didn't get to the unconscious guard before he woke, her subterfuge would be pointless and Merrick would be caught before he'd gotten more than a mile down the road.

Emerging into the clearing, she saw one of Brandt's guards laying spread-eagle in the grass near a stone bench. To her consternation, she noticed a small dart protruding from his neck. Shuddering in distaste, she plucked it free and tossed it in some nearby bushes.

After assuring herself that no one had noticed

the exchange—at least, no one had raised an alarm—she took a seat and pulled a handful of pins from a small pocket she'd sewn into her gown. Sweeping her hair into a similar style to the one Alyssa had worn, she carefully anchored the veil in place before arranging the layers of lace and tulle so it completely concealed her features. And just in time. At her feet, the guard stirred.

"What…"

She swiftly crouched beside him, silver chiffon skirting flaring around her. "Are you okay?" she asked in a soft voice, praying she sounded similar to Princess Alyssa. Why, oh, why, hadn't she asked Merrick to make the woman speak so she'd have a better idea of accent and intonation? It was a foolish mistake. "You tripped or passed out or something. Are you ill? Should I call your superior and tell him you fainted?"

A dull red swept across the man's cheekbones and alarm filled his brown eyes. "No, no, ma'am. I'm fine."

"I think they want us inside." She slipped a shoulder beneath his arm and helped him to his feet, which only increased the spread of embarrassed red across his broad features. "Are you sure you don't need help? Maybe I should request a doctor for you."

"Please." His voice lowered to a whisper. "Don't tell anyone this happened. It could mean my position in the Guard."

"Oh, dear. That would be terrible." She infused a wealth of sympathy in her voice. "I'll tell you what. We'll keep it our secret. After all, no harm done. I'm right here, safe and sound."

The guard nodded in relief. "Yes, Your Highness. I'm grateful that you didn't attempt to run off when the opportunity presented itself."

Run off? Her brows pulled together. Why would the guard suspect Alyssa might run, unless… Miri's breathing hitched. The comment suggested that Princess Alyssa wasn't a cooperative bride, that the guard wasn't here as an honorary attendant, but in an official military capacity. But why? What was going on? Was Brandt forcing the marriage? Her eyes closed in anguish. If so, why was he doing it? Was he so desperate to be king that nothing else mattered?

She found that difficult to believe. She knew Brandt. He wasn't like that. She couldn't equate the man who'd go to such extreme measures with the one she'd known since the tender age of seven, let alone the Brandt of one short month ago. Tears pricked her eyes. The Brandt she'd fallen in love with.

"Of course I didn't run off," she murmured. "After all, where would I go?"

Together they crossed to the gateway separating the expanse of garden from the inner courtyard of the chapel. Guards formed a corridor of uniformed muscle from gateway to chapel entry and she ran the gauntlet without a word. She stumbled as she entered the vestibule, blinded by a combination of the dim interior and the heavily tatted veil.

Her escort slipped a hand beneath her arm, steadying her. "Your Highness?"

"I'm fine, thank you," she murmured.

A bevy of bridesmaids in a rainbow of pastels surrounded her briefly, before reorganizing themselves into pairs for their trip up the aisle. One fluttered to Miri's side, dipped a curtsey and handed her a bouquet of cascading calla lilies, the lilac color a beautiful complement to the silver tone of her gown. It made her want to cry. This should have been real. This should have been her wedding day. It shouldn't have been this…this lie.

Why, Brandt?

Drawing a deep breath, she moved to stand beneath the archway that led into the sanctuary. At her appearance, a massive pipe organ thundered out the first few triumphant notes of a wedding march prelude. She knew she was supposed to move forward, to take slow, gliding steps up the aisle. Instead, she stared at the man standing, waiting, in front of the altar.

He made for a striking figure. Tall. Commanding. Ebony-eyed with hair as dark as a starless night, no one would have labeled him as handsome. Not like Merrick and Lander. Brandt's features were too austere for conventional good looks, the planes and angles of his face hard and uncompromising. Intimidating. Until he smiled. When he did that, his entire expression changed.

And that's what he'd done when they'd run into each other right before King Stefan's death. He'd smiled at her and she'd fallen. No, not fallen. Tumbled, helplessly, endlessly, passionately, forever in love. She thought he'd felt the same, that he loved her every bit as much, and she'd planned to go to his bed, to allow what she felt for him to take physical expression. But before they could consummate their relationship, she'd received the call informing her of her stepfather's death, and had immediately flown home.

To her eternal shame, she'd left Brandt a note. One almost incoherent in its odd combination of love and grief. In that note she'd detailed, in no uncertain terms, precisely how she felt about him along with her hopes and dreams for their future, painting her childish picture in broad, vibrant, adoring strokes. What a fool she'd been!

She glared at the man waiting for her at the altar. That's what came from being so impulsive—a character trait she'd never been able to overcome—and for flinging herself headlong at a man who saw life in shades of gray, never in color. A man without emotions, who put ambition ahead of everything else. Tears threatened and Miri forced aside the pain and anguish in favor of anger, needing that blinding fury in order to hold all other emotions at bay and get through this next hideous hour.

Taking a deep breath, she moved forward,

heading step by step toward a revenge she'd never thought herself capable of. And all the while memories washed over her. Memories of how it had all started.

She was a fool. A total and utter fool.

Here it was well past midnight and she'd managed to lose the group of friends she'd been vacationing with on the tiny Caribbean island of Mazoné. They'd all gone to the grand opening of a new club that had been tucked a few blocks off the main drag. It wasn't until she'd enjoyed several hours of dancing that she'd discovered she'd lost them. By then the noise and crowd had become overwhelming and she'd decided to head back to the hotel on her own.

It had been a huge mistake. She'd never been accused of having much sense of direction when she actually knew where she was going. In a strange city, late at night, she'd managed to prove to herself just how bad it was. She'd headed out, certain she knew the way back to her hotel. But in just a few short blocks, the ambiance had gone from upscale party scene to dark and threatening. Worst of all, she hadn't a clue how to get back to where she belonged.

She clipped down the street in a ridiculous pair of four-inch heels at a I-know-where-I'm-going-don't-bug-me pace, praying she'd come across whatever served as local law enforcement, a cab, or a knight on a white charger. Even a knight *in* a white charger would do. Anyone who could point her in the right direction or—better yet—escort her there.

Instead of any of those things, she heard a noise that sent chills shooting through her, the scurry of stealthy footsteps, rapidly approaching. The sound echoed through the empty streets behind her, her first warning of impending danger. And then came confirmation that she was in serious trouble, a single voice that commanded, "Get her!"

Without hesitation, Miri hastened around the next corner she came to, kicked off her heels and took off running. Adrenaline screamed through her system, threatening to numb her mind. Her heart pounded so loudly she couldn't hear over the desperate thrumming. Were they still behind her? Closing? A sob choked her, making it difficult to breathe. She fought against the fear, fought against caving to sheer panic, fought even harder to remember everything Merrick had taught her about self-defense.

She forced herself to focus. Elbows. Elbows were the strongest point on her body. If her attacker got close enough, she'd use them. Then nails to the eyes. A fist to the nose. But first she'd toss her purse toward them, hoping that would satisfy long enough for her to get away. The credit cards and few dollars she had on her could be replaced.

Other things couldn't.

Rounding another corner, she ran straight into a wall of muscle. *Oh, God. Please, please, please! Don't let this be happening.* Somehow they'd surrounded her, cutting her off front and behind. Bouncing backward a couple steps, she tossed back her waist-length hair so it wouldn't impede her and threw a punch—one the man casually blocked. So was her knee to his groin and her elbow to his midsection. Each countermove was accomplished with an economy of movement and a smooth grace that spoke of long practice. The realization that she didn't have a chance against this man filled her with unmitigated terror. She opened her mouth to scream, but to her horror all that escaped was a pathetic whimper. Parrying a final blow, the man caught both of her wrists in his hands with terrifying ease.

She twisted her arms in an attempt to break his hold, an exercise in sheer futility. "Please—" The word escaped in a sob. "Let me go."

CHAPTER TWO

"RELAX." The man's voice rumbled from six full inches above her. "I won't hurt you."

"Then let me go." She spared a swift glance over her shoulder. "Please!"

"Stop fighting me and I will."

A thread of amusement drifted through his comment, and there was something about his voice that struck a chord deep inside, some quality that she would have recognized if she weren't so terrified. Before she had an opportunity to respond, footsteps skittered behind her. It had to be whoever had been chasing her earlier. They came to an abrupt stop when they caught sight of her and who she was with, and hovered uncertainly. The man holding her released her wrists. Sweeping her behind him, he turned to confront her pursuers.

"Don't be afraid. I'll take care of this," he murmured. Raising his voice, he called to them. "This little one is mine now. Turn around and walk away and I won't have to hurt you."

She peeked out from behind his back, wincing when she saw there wasn't just one or two, but three of them. Heaven help her! She wouldn't have stood a chance. They shifted and bobbed, reminding of her of a pack of hyenas working up the nerve to attack.

"Maybe I'll just run," she offered apprehensively.

He shook his head. "They'd only give chase."

She heard it again, that quality in his voice. But before she could analyze it, he glanced over his shoulder at her. She caught a brief glimpse of a hard, hawklike profile and the glitter of cold, determined dark eyes. It matched the rest of him and she shivered, realizing that this man could very well prove more dangerous than all three at the end of the block combined.

He had Lander's impressive height, but was built more like Merrick. Lean and sinewy, she could feel tense, well-defined muscles through the jacket of his tux. Why hadn't she noticed before? He was wearing a *tux.* She supposed there could be the occasional well-dressed assailant out there. But she seriously doubted anyone interested in offering her harm would run around attacking women while wearing formal wear. For the first time since she'd gotten herself into this mess, she breathed a little easier. But only for a moment.

The three men at the end of the block were talking quietly. At a guess, they were discussing their options. Maybe working up their courage. She knew the instant they'd reached a decision. In unison, their heads swiveled toward her, their smiles shining bleached-bone white in the darkness. As one they came, swift and assured, forming a wide half circle as they moved forward. A pack of predators circling their prey.

The man she cowered behind didn't so much as twitch. He simply stood and waited. "Aren't you going to do something?" she asked nervously, plucking at the back of his tux jacket. "Maybe we should run."

"Do as I say and you won't get hurt. Stay behind me and keep out of the way." He shot her a swift warning look. "Don't run."

Right before the three were on top of them she caught the distinct flash of steel in each of their hands. She called out a warning—ridiculous, as well as pointless, considering he could see far better than she what they held. Nor did her warning do any good. He still didn't react. The assailants took two more swift steps forward and that's when the man protecting her responded. The explosion of movement lasted less than thirty seconds. A short, chopping blow. A kick. A punch. And all three were down, sprawled in a disjointed heap while their weapons clattered discordantly to the pavement.

Pivoting, the man dropped an arm around her shoulders and urged her away from the scene. As soon as he realized she was shoeless, he slowed the pace and helped her avoid anything that might cut or injure her feet. "Where do you belong?" He ushered her down a dark alleyway and onto a street that actually held traffic. Up ahead she could see the welcome glow of lights. "What's the name of your hotel?"

She swallowed against the dryness in her throat, struggling to get her brain functioning again and her breathing slowed now that the crisis was over. "I'm staying at the Carlton," she said, naming the only five-star hotel on the island.

He inclined his head in a courtly manner. It was one she'd seen countless times before at royal functions and public occasions, and one that held her riveted. "As am I."

And that's when it hit her, why his voice had

struck such a chord, why even his manner-isms seemed familiar. "I know that accent. You're Verdonian!" They stepped from shadow into light and she caught her first good look at him. "Brandt." His name escaped in a soft gasp of wonder and delight. The realization that she'd escaped almost certain disaster without injury—thanks to this man, no less—made her almost giddy with relief. She'd always consid-ered him a knight in shining armor. Tonight he'd proved it. "Brandt! It is you, isn't it? Don't you recognize me? It's me. Miri Montgomery."

Brandt stared at her, not quite able to equate the awkward teen he vaguely remembered with this vibrant, gorgeous woman he'd just rescued. "Miri?"

"Oh, thank you." Lifting onto tiptoe, she threw her arms around his neck and kissed first one cheek and then the other, before planting a gentle, lingering kiss on his mouth. Her lips were petal-soft and warm, not quite as skilled as his last lover's, but experienced enough to know what she was doing—and what she was offering. Pulling back, she gave him a broad smile. "Thank you so much for saving me."

His hands settled at her waist, a tiny waist covered by a mere slip of a dress. Damn it! She was practically naked. What the hell was she thinking, running around like that? And who had let this…this *child* loose in one of the most dangerous sections of Mazoné? When he found out, he'd make the man regret it to his dying day. Instead of returning her smile, he frowned in disapproval. "What are you doing here, Miri?"

"I'm on vacation." She slipped her hand through his arm in a companionable gesture, seemingly unaware of the way her grasp pressed her breasts tight against his sleeve. "How about you?"

He fought not to react to her as a woman. It wasn't right. She was practically family, not to mention far too young. "No, I mean, what were you doing in the part of town where I found you? You could have been hurt…or worse."

"I got lost."

Anger vied with concern. "Where's your family? Where are your brothers? Who's looking out for you?"

She blinked up at him. As soon as she registered his annoyance, her chin rose and she gave him a level stare from bottle-green eyes. He'd forgotten how stunning those eyes were, how they reflected her every thought and emotion. Confusion. Irritation. Affront. "I'm looking out for myself," she replied evenly. "It's been so long since we last saw each other, you've probably forgotten there's only seven years between us, Brandt. I turn twenty-five next month."

Was it possible? Had so many years passed since he'd last seen her? His gaze swept over her once again, seeing the woman who'd ripened from the child he remembered. It only served to fuel his anger. "That makes you old enough to know better than to wander through a dangerous section of town at two in the morning without an escort."

She waved that aside. "I'm old enough to take care of myself."

"Is that what you were doing when you were running from those men? Taking care of yourself?"

She released his arm and dipped into a practiced curtsey, somehow managing to imbue it with amused sarcasm. "You always did do intimidation well, Your Highness. Tonight you excel at it." Her smile flashed again. "Come on, Brandt, stop acting like my hidebound old uncle. You're not. Nor do I want you to be."

He lifted an eyebrow. If she found him intimidating, she didn't show it. He'd have to see what he could do about that. He approached, crowding her. "What would you have done when those three caught you?"

Without shoes, she barely cleared his shoulders. She tilted back her head and a waterfall of silky black hair swirled around her hips.

"I'd have scratched their eyes out. Kicked. Screamed." She shrugged. "Merrick taught me how to defend myself."

"Yes, it worked so well with me." He deliberately caught her wrists in his, as he'd done earlier, holding her with ease. "And I didn't even have a knife."

He scored with that one. She flinched as though she could still see those knives gleaming in the moonlight. Hell, he could still see them. Wickedly serrated. Purposeful. Glittering with the promise of serious injury, if not death. The thought of them scoring her tender flesh made him want to howl in fury. She wouldn't have stood a chance against the three who'd been chasing her, even if they hadn't been armed.

Something of his thoughts must have shown in his face and for the first time she did appear intimidated. "Let go, Brandt."

"Make me. Prove you could have defended yourself against even one man."

Instead of fighting him, she stepped forward and rested her forehead against his chest, leaning into him. "You're right. I couldn't have." She sounded exhausted. "Let me say it again. Seriously, this time. Thank you for saving my life. I do know that if you hadn't been there, tonight would have ended far differently."

Her words hit like a blow, succeeding where defiance never would have. Releasing her wrists, he forked his fingers deep into the rich mass of her hair and tilted her head upward. The moonlight caught in her eyes, turning them iridescent. "I wouldn't want anything to happen to you. I'd never forgive myself." His mouth tilted to one side. "I doubt your family would, either."

Instead of pulling free, she continued to stand within his grasp, her body locked tight against his. "Do you know that I was madly in love with you when I was a child?" she asked him with an impulsiveness he'd always found disconcerting. "Wildly, crazily, deliciously in love, or as much as a child can be. Crazy, huh?"

For the first time that evening his features relaxed and a found himself smiling. "Were you now?" Unable to resist, he traced the curve of her cheek with his thumb. The smooth, creamy skin proved as soft to the touch as it looked. "You always were a reckless child. I'm not sure much has changed since then."

"Maybe not," she conceded with a shrug. "One thing's changed, though."

"And what's that?"

She grinned up at him. "In case you haven't noticed, I'm not a child anymore."

He couldn't help it. His gaze wandered over her, taking in the short, spangled dress, wishing he could do more than look. He wanted to gather her up and carry her back to the hotel. Even more, he wanted to strip away that handful of silk and bare her. Touch her. Take her. No matter how wrong it might be. He did none of those things, allowed none of what he felt to show in his expression. Gently, he set her away from him.

"You're right," he murmured. "You are all grown up. But this isn't the time or place. Let's get you to your hotel."

"Okay."

Instead of stepping back and continuing on toward the Carlton, she tilted her head to one side and held him with those clear mountain-lake eyes, eyes that reflected a desire so strong, it roused the most primal instincts he possessed, instincts that demanded he take what she so blatantly offered. Take here and now, giving no quarter. How he managed to hold himself in check, he never recalled.

Tucking her hand into the crook of his arm once again, she gave him a final verbal shove, one that shot him straight over the edge. "So, tell me, Brandt," she said as casually as though they were discussing the weather. "When and where would be the right time and place? I want time, date and location, if you don't mind. I want to finish what we've started."

The memory faded and Brandt forced himself to watch his bride drift toward him while the pipe organ thundered out the processional, as though volume could drown out what everyone gathered today whispered—that this ceremony was little more than a farce. His gloved hands collapsed into fists before he forcibly relaxed them.

Those whispers were all too accurate, not that it made him any happier about the situation. As for his memories of Miri and those amazing weeks together, they were just that. Memories. Bittersweet moments-out-of-time that were no longer possible and never could be again. He fixed his attention on his bride and kept it there. He couldn't afford to lose focus, not when so much depended on him.

Princess Alyssa approached, not a scrap of her visible beneath a traditional Verdonian veil of lace and tulle. Just as well, all things considered. All he needed to make this travesty complete was a bride weeping her way through the ceremony, something Angela, the mother of the bride, was handling quite capably, thank you very much.

The organ music continued even after the bride had reached his side, creating an awkward few minutes. Finally, it died away and the ceremony began. The minute Alyssa opened her mouth to whisper the vows being forced on her, Brandt thanked divine intervention for her voluminous veil. She didn't sound at all like herself, whether from anger or tears he couldn't quite tell, but he'd just as soon not have to witness either one.

When his turn came to speak his vows, he did so without hesitation in a calm, carrying voice that held not a scrap of emotion. Duty didn't require emotion. And he did have a duty. A burdensome one. To the principality he governed.

To the country he loved more than himself. But especially to the people of that country.

No matter how much he might wish this bride were someone far different than Alyssa Sutherland—in fact, a woman almost her polar opposite—that choice had been taken from him when he received the reports about the Montgomerys' malfeasance. They'd stolen from Verdonia, from the country they'd sworn to protect. After that, there had been no other choice available to him except this one. And he'd fulfill his responsibilities, no matter how distasteful he found them.

With a start he realized the brief ceremony was drawing to a close, the benediction gravely intoned over their bowed heads. Next came the traditional declaration of their union, words of permanence that held endless complications. "From this day forward, until the end of your reign on this earth, may you forever and ever remain husband and wife." A pause followed, a pointed acknowledgement of the pragmatic nature of the ceremony just performed, before the final words of the ceremony were pronounced. "Your Highness, you may kiss your bride."

Brandt reached for Alyssa's veil, but she took an unexpected step backward, her hand pressed to her middle. "Please," she whispered. "I don't feel well. I think I'm going to be sick."

Perfect. The perfect end to a perfect wedding. Just as well. He had no more desire to kiss her than she had to kiss him. As a way out, illness worked fine for him. He turned to the congregation with a calm smile. "My bride knows Verdonian tradition well. She has requested that I unveil her in private, so I'm the first to set eyes on her as my wife."

There was a wave of uncertain laughter drowned out by a recessional more thunderous than the processional. Offering his arm to Alyssa, Brandt escorted her down the aisle, through the vestibule, and into the sun-dappled courtyard. Off to one side, a small wooden doorway stood ajar and, without waiting for an escort, he led her into the tunnel that ran from chapel to palace.

"Hold on just a few minutes longer," he murmured. "We'll get you to your room."

"Thank you."

The words echoed strangely in the tunnels, softening the broad American tones that normally flavored her voice. He couldn't help comparing it to a different sort of accent, still American-born, but with an underlying hint of a Verdonian lilt. Teasing. Impulsive. Filled with laughter. Just the sound of it had broken through layers of pomp and circumstance, allowing him to feel human, if only for those brief days he'd spent on Mazoné.

The tunnel emerged at a central courtyard in the palace and he escorted Alyssa—his *wife,* he forcibly corrected himself—to a doorway that connected the courtyard to a corridor not far from the suite of rooms he'd given her, rooms that adjoined his own. She would have disappeared inside without a word or backward look, if he hadn't stopped her with a hand to her shoulder.

Alyssa froze beneath his hold. "Don't" was all she said.

"I know you want an explanation."

She spun to face him, her illness apparently forgotten, assuming she'd been feeling sick in the first place. "Yes, I would."

"And I also explained that I couldn't give you one. Not yet. I'm sorry, Alyssa."

He could feel the frustration radiating off her. "So am I. You must want to be king very badly."

Hell. He should have known he couldn't keep that quiet. "Who's been speaking to you about that?"

"No one. I just assumed…"

"You claimed not to know anything about Verdonia's political situation," he cut in. "Or was that a lie?"

Her hands wrapped themselves in the folds

of her gown, betraying her nervousness. "It's just something one of my bridesmaids said," she murmured. "I don't understand how marrying me will accomplish your goal to be king, but apparently it does."

"It's complicated."

"Why don't you uncomplicate it?"

He stilled. Up until now Alyssa had always been soft-spoken. Almost timid. The only time she'd confronted him had been out of concern for her mother's safety, one of the more despicable methods he'd used to coerce Alyssa into this travesty of a marriage. Though it was something he'd spend the rest of life regretting, he deliberately shoved the memory away, compartmentalizing it for another time, after he'd met his duties and obligations.

She must have realized she'd said something wrong because she edged away from him, pressing her back to the door. "I'm sorry. I shouldn't have asked. I'm not feeling well and I'm upset."

"You deserve to know, Alyssa." He reached past her, trying not to take it personally when she flinched from him. "Go on in your room and rest. I'll send your mother to you."

"No! Please don't bother her."

Now he was certain something was wrong. His eyes narrowed. "You've done nothing but ask to see her since you arrived. Now that you can, you don't want to?"

"I…I—"

"Alyssa? Baby?" Angela appeared at the far end of the corridor and hurried toward them. "Are you all right?"

"Fine, er, Mom. I'm fine."

Brandt shoved the door open and gestured to the two women. "Why don't we go inside where we'll have a little more privacy."

Since he had both women together, he'd take the time to explain as much as he could about the current political situation in Verdonia. He signaled to a pair of his men stationed nearby.

Immediately, they took up positions on either side of the doorway.

Once closeted inside Alyssa's suite, he regarded his wife and mother-in-law. The two stood next to each other, speaking in soft murmurs. To his consternation, Angela looked ready to burst into tears again. She kept darting swift, apprehensive looks from him to her daughter and every scrap of color had fled her cheeks. Hell. What a predicament.

Crossing the room, he tried not to take offense when the two stiffened in alarm. He caught the trailing end of Alyssa's veil and lifted it. "Here. Let's get this off you. I'm sure you'll be more comfortable without it."

CHAPTER THREE

"No!" Miri snatched the veil from Brandt's grasp. "Don't." She backed away, tripping over the hem of her gown in her haste. "I'd rather keep it on."

His eyes narrowed in blatant suspicion. He sensed something was wrong, and if she didn't act fast, he'd figure it out. She was amazed he hadn't already. Some problem must have him preoccupied, otherwise a man as intelligent as Brandt would have put two and two together by now.

Angela had known instantly she wasn't Alyssa. It had only taken two words for mother to tell an imposter from her daughter. Thank goodness Brandt didn't know his wife quite so well. And thank goodness he'd given the two women a few seconds for private conversation. It hadn't given her much time, but it had been long enough to reassure Angela that her daughter was safe and beg the poor woman to remain silent about the switch.

Miri fought to regain her focus. Okay, one problem at a time. The most pressing concern was to distract Brandt while keeping her veil firmly on her head. "Please…I think I'm coming down with a migraine." She did her best to mimic Angela's voice, in the hopes it would sound similar to Alyssa's. People had always thought Miri's voice identical to her mother, Rachel's, and often confused them on the phone. With luck, the same held true with Alyssa and her mother. Based on Angela's amazed reaction, the attempt must have passed muster. "I get headaches sometimes when I'm stressed. Noise and light make them worse. The veil is actually helping."

"Migraine," Angela parroted, babbling nervously. "Please, she needs to keep her veil on."

Judging by Brandt's expression, he didn't believe her excuse for a single minute. To her relief, he didn't press the issue. With a shrug, he stepped back, giving the two women some breathing space. "If it makes you more comfortable to leave it on, that's fine," he said to Miri.

The gentleness of his voice had her blinking in surprise. Did he attribute her insistence that she remain veiled to fear? If so, she'd run with it. "Thank you. I feel so much better with it on."

She shot a quick glance in Angela's direction in the hopes of gaining some hint as to how to proceed. But the woman stood transfixed, staring in blatant panic, so Miri spun to confront Brandt. No, not confront. Clearly, that wasn't typical of how Alyssa had dealt with him up to this point. She'd ask. Politely.

"Please, Your Highness. You promised to explain what's going on to me and my mother." She crossed to Angela's side and took the woman's trembling hand in hers. "Why did you force me to marry you?"

He folded his arms across his chest and contemplated the two women. "I need your mother's assistance in order to get all the facts straight."

Miri spared Angela a swift glance. She looked on the verge of passing out. "What does my mother have to do with any of this?"

"She needs to tell you who you are. You haven't, have you?" he asked the older woman.

Angela shook her head, her breath escaping in a shuddering sigh. "She doesn't know anything."

"If I may?" He waited for her reluctant nod before continuing. "What your mother has neglected to tell you is that you were born Princess Alyssa Sutherland, here in Verdonia. You're the daughter of Prince Frederick, who died a few years ago, and the half sister of his son, Erik. When you were a year old your mother divorced your father and left the country with you."

Okay, if she were really Alyssa, she'd be surprised by this information. "Is this true?" she demanded of her "mother."

"Yes." Angela's grip on Miri's hand spasmed. "I'm sorry I didn't tell you before."

"Why? Why didn't you?"

Angela caught her bottom lip between her teeth. "I just wanted to start over. To leave my past in the past." She shot a reproachful glare in Brandt's direction. "That didn't work very well."

"No, it didn't," Miri agreed. "Which leads me to my next question. What has my heritage got to do with—" Her gesture encompassed Brandt and the palace around them. "With why I'm here and our marriage?"

He frowned as though debating what to say next. "Do you know anything about how Verdonia's monarchy works?"

Miri hesitated and sent another quick glance

in Angela's direction, who hastened to answer the question. "I haven't told her anything about that, either."

Brandt nodded, as though not surprised. "I'll see if I can keep this simple." He crossed to the writing desk positioned in one corner of the room and helped himself to a piece of paper and pen. Drawing a rough map of the country, he handed it to Miri. "Verdonia is divided into three principalities, each ruled by its own prince or princess. The northernmost principality—mine—is Avernos. The central one is Celestia, where your brother, Erik, most recently ruled. And the southernmost is Verdon and is governed by Lander Montgomery."

"Go on."

"Unlike most monarchies, we elect our kings and queens by popular vote from the three royal bloodlines, rather than allowing the crown to pass along hereditary lines. Until six weeks ago, we were ruled by King Stefan Montgomery. With his death, the people of Verdonia will choose his successor from the eldest eligible prince and princess of each principality."

"Are you one?" She already knew the answer, but it seemed an appropriate question.

"Yes."

"Am I?" Another reasonable question, one she'd neglected to ask Merrick and one he hadn't thought to volunteer. Though perhaps he hadn't known for certain.

Brandt shook his head. "Normally, your brother, Erik, would have been a candidate. But he abdicated his position immediately after King Stefan's death. Though you're qualified at any age to govern your particular principality—in this case, Celestia—you're not eligible to rule all of Verdonia because you won't be twenty-five at the time of the election."

She'd heard about Erik's abdication, if not the reason for it. A question for Merrick once she got out of here. "What I still don't understand is why the marriage? You haven't explained that part."

"Since neither you nor Erik is eligible to rule Verdonia, the choice is between me and Lander Montgomery." His dark eyes lost all expression, his voice taking on an emotionless quality. "Remember we're dealing with a popular ballot. Our citizens tend to vote the prince or princess from their principality. That means Verdon will throw in with Lander, and Avernos with me. If it were just a contest between the two of us, Montgomery would win since the population of Verdon is largest. But there's still Celestia to consider."

Even a child could figure out where this was headed. "Whichever way Celestia votes, so votes the country." The map crumpled in her hand. "Because of our marriage, Celestia will want to remain loyal to its princess and vote for her husband—namely, you. Celestia plus Avernos equals a crown."

"Yes."

Tears filled her eyes at the unapologetic acknowledgement. She'd been so certain there was more involved in his decision than simple greed. How could she have been so mistaken about the man she loved? "Then the woman I overheard is right," she stated numbly. "You married me to be king."

He didn't bother to deny it. "Yes," he said again.

"You bastard." The accusation came out in a low hiss, full of feminine fury. "How dare you?"

Angela stepped hurriedly between them. "My daughter isn't feeling well. Please. Could you give her some time to rest? I'm sure her headache will be better in a few hours."

Brandt inclined his head. "Yes. I'm sure it will. Unfortunately, we need to deal with this here and now, headache or no." He glanced at Angela. "Would you excuse us, please? You and Alyssa can spend the day together tomorrow and get caught up then. Today…your daughter and I need to come to terms."

It was clear Angela didn't want to leave,

and equally clear she couldn't bring herself to confront him. "Yes, Your Highness," she murmured after an extended pause. Sparing Miri a single anguished look, she exited the room.

Brandt approached, silent and determined, and Miri took a hasty step backward, not that it did any good. Taking her forcibly by the hand, he lifted her fingers and brushed them with his mouth. "None of what I've told you changes anything."

"You have to be kidding," she protested, remembering just in time to alter the sound of her voice. "It changes everything."

"I warned you what I expected from this marriage. And the first thing I expect is to find you recovered by this evening."

Her eyes widened. Surely he didn't mean… Even through the dense layers of lace and tulle she could see his expression well enough to know he meant precisely that. "Oh, no." Maybe the veil gave her the courage to be so confrontational. Under normal circumstances, she'd have watched her tongue. "That is *not* going to happen. No way, no how."

He simply smiled. "I warned you before that this would be a real marriage. Nothing has changed since then."

"Everything's changed. You're using me to win the throne. That's outrageous!" She kicked her skirts out of her way as she strode across the room. "I notice you were careful to keep that detail from me before the wedding."

"For cause."

She paused before him, relieved that he couldn't see her expression, that he couldn't see the grief and anguish glittering in her eyes. "You married me for cause," she repeated. "What cause? Explain it to me. Explain that there's something more going on than some clever plan to steal the throne."

Anger shredded his emotionless facade. "I'm not stealing the throne."

"No? What do you call it?"

"Saving Verdonia from the Montgomerys."

She flinched as though he'd slapped her. "I don't understand."

"And I can't explain. Not yet. Just trust me when I say that it wouldn't be in Verdonia's best interest to have another Montgomery on the throne."

"You're doing this to ensure Prince Lander isn't elected king?" He fell silent at the question and Miri knew from experience she wouldn't get any more out of him. Still, she had to try. Any information she could bring back to Merrick would be useful, possibly vital. "Has he offended you in some way? Caused some sort of trouble that would have an adverse effect on Verdonia?"

He simply shook his head. "Eventually I'll be able to justify my actions. And I promise, you'll agree there's cause for concern. In the meantime, we have more important issues to deal with." He smiled, a slow curve of his lips that had melted her on more occasions than she could count. Even now, she could feel that smile working and struggled to steel herself against its pull. "Today's our wedding day. I'd like to see if we can't find a way to make our marriage work."

She wanted to agree, until she remembered that he wasn't speaking to her, but to Alyssa Sutherland. His *wife,* or at least the woman he thought he'd married. Miri took a deep breath. "I'm supposed to forgive what you put me through? What you've done to my…my mother? I'm supposed to forget about all that and turn into a happy, eager bride? You've lost your mind, if you think that's going to happen."

"I wouldn't have hurt her or you. I forced the issue because it was urgent that we marry."

"For the good of Verdonia."

"Yes."

More than anything Miri wanted to drag off her veil and confront him as herself. To demand an explanation. But that wasn't possible. There was more at stake here than assuaging her pride. She struggled to draw a decent breath, feeling smothered beneath the layers covering her. Not just smothered, but tired and hurt, too. Crossing the room, she sank into the nearest chair.

"I need some time alone." She lifted her hands to rub her temples before realizing she couldn't. "I really do have a headache."

"Very well." He indicated the door next to her chair. "If you need me, I'll be in my room. I've arranged for a tray to be delivered in a few minutes, just some tea and a light snack."

"Thank you."

He approached, standing far too close. "And I've ordered a private dinner for later this evening. I'll expect you to join me." He touched the trailing edge of her veil. "Without this."

He didn't bother to wait for her response, which was just as well, since she had none to offer. The minute the door closed behind him, Miri burst into tears. It was a foolish indulgence, but one she couldn't seem to prevent. She gave herself two full minutes to cry it out, then another minute to regain her composure, all the while forcing herself to face facts. She'd learned as much as she could from Brandt. It was time to get out of here.

A soft knock sounded at the door leading to the outer corridor and a maid peeked into the room. Seeing Miri sitting there, she slipped in, carrying a tray. "Tea and sandwiches, Your Highness. Shall I serve you?"

"No, thank you," Miri murmured. "Just leave them, please."

The girl had been well-trained. With a minimal amount of fuss, she arranged the contents of the tray on a nearby table, and with a quick curtsey, exited the room. The instant Miri was alone again, she ripped the veil from her head. Tangled streams of hair tumbled free of the pins, the sight of those sunny blond curls threatening more tears. The color was a painful reminder that the man she loved had chosen someone else, someone who looked as different from her as night from day.

She would have sworn her time with Brandt on Mazoné had been serious, that he was incapable of the type of cold-blooded acts he'd committed over the past several weeks. Her jaw firmed. But now she knew the truth. Brandt had married to be king. He'd married to prevent her brother from gaining the throne. Standing here weeping over might-have-beens was both pointless, as well as foolish. She needed to leave. Now.

Crossing to the walk-in closet on the far side of the room, she yanked open the doors. She found the selection less than impressive. Alyssa hadn't come to Verdonia with much of a wardrobe. Either she'd planned to replace it when she'd arrived, or she hadn't planned to stay long. Miri's mouth tightened. Until Brandt had changed her mind.

Flipping through the choices she selected a plain navy skirt and ivory shell. Not quite the sort of finery a guest would have worn to a wedding, but it should pass muster for getting her out of here as Miri Montgomery. She slipped the clothing from the hangers and draped them over the chair before reaching for her zipper. It was then that she remembered her gown didn't have a zipper. Not a zipper or buttons, or any other easy way out of her clothing.

She'd forgotten she'd been sewn into the darn thing, as tradition dictated, the workmanship too skillful to even rip her way free. Someone would need to help. Either that or she'd have to find a pair of scissors or a knife and cut her way out. Her gaze drifted toward the table where her meal waited, the gleam of silver catching her eye. Hurrying over, she examined the utensils. Sure enough, there was a knife, but a blunt one lacking even the hint of a serrated edge, intended for nothing more onerous than buttering bread.

It was the last straw. Sinking into the chair, she buried her face in her hands. More than anything, she wanted to go back to how it had been before her stepfather had died, to those amazing carefree weeks when her day revolved around falling in love with Brandt. Most of all, she wanted to return to that last perfect day they'd shared on Mazoné. To go back and relive those final happy moments over and over again.

"How far is this place?" she panted.

"Not far," Brandt replied. "We just need to follow this river up into the mountain a short way."

Scrambling behind him, Miri paused at the next outcropping of rocks to gaze at the heavy foliage that tumbled down the mountainside in an unbroken cascade of green. The river flowed beside the path they took, chattering over heavy black boulders on its passage to the ocean. Ferns and lianas overflowed the banks, while huge flower blossoms peeked at them with faces containing a variety of shades more spectacular than a rainbow. A flock of parakeets burst from the brush on one side and streamed in a flash of yellow, blue and green through a gateway of orange heliconia that bordered the far side of the stream.

"Move it, Montgomery. You can't be out of breath already."

The path drifted deeper into the jungle from where she stood, away from the river. Wiping the perspiration from her face, she hiked up the last forty feet. But when she'd reached the spot she'd last seen Brandt, he was nowhere to be found. "Hey, where'd you go?"

"Through here."

His voice came from the direction of the river, well off the path. Shoving past endless ferns and palm fronds, she stepped into a clearing and stopped dead. Wordless, she simply stared. To her left, a fifty-foot cliff towered above them, the river pouring off it in a silver sheet to form a wide circular pool at their feet. A narrow channel to her right sent the river continuing on its way downstream. Flowers and foliage grew in and around the tumble of rocks, forming a brilliant explosion of color.

But most glorious of all were the butterflies. Hundreds of them floated in the misty air, like flower petals swirling on an endless updraft. She'd never seen such a riot of color before, luminous jewels of every hue given flight on iridescent wings.

Brandt grinned at her amazement. "What are you waiting for? Strip, woman." He lifted an eyebrow at her hesitation. "You are wearing a bathing suit under your clothes, aren't you?"

"Yes, of course."

"Too bad."

Miri choked on a laugh, but her amusement didn't last long, fading beneath an intense longing she couldn't disguise. Not from herself, nor from Brandt. She wanted him, had wanted him almost as long as she could remember. Her gaze locked with his and without a word she kicked off her shoes and slipped off her shorts and tee, allowing them to puddle at her feet. He followed suit.

Then, he took her hand in his, holding it for an impossibly long moment. It was a large, strong hand with powerfully corded ligaments and tendons that were far more suited to a laborer than a pencil pusher. He held her with tempered strength, the moment stretching before he helped her into the pool.

The next hour passed like a dream, the two of them playing and splashing in the water together. Laughter rang across the glade. Finally, exhausted, they levered themselves up onto a flat rock close to the waterfall. A soft spray misted them, cool and refreshing beneath the hot Caribbean sun. Miri sat cross-legged on the rock, combing her fingers through her hair.

To her surprise, Brandt's hands joined hers, working with her to free the tangles. "I wish…I wish I could stay in this moment forever." She tilted her head to watch the colorful dance above them. "The butterflies. The waterfall. The flowers and pool and—" Her voice dropped. "And you."

"I've discovered nothing lasts forever, no matter how much I might want it otherwise."

"That sounds like something your grandfather would have said."

Brandt shrugged. "Not surprising considering he raised me."

"As I recall, he had a saying for every occasion, especially when I'd get into trouble." She shifted in place at the memory. "He made me so nervous the first time I met him."

"Finally. Someone who intimidates you."

"Cut me some slack. I was all of seven. My mom had just married King Stefan and I was feeling very much out of my element. Then I literally ran into this tall, gruff man at one of Verdonia's royal functions, a man who looked even more like a king than my stepfather. How would you feel?"

Brandt lifted an eyebrow. "I assume you weren't intimidated for long."

"Heavens no. Not once I got past his tough exterior to the marshmallow center." She smiled fondly. "Your grandfather was very kind to me. Gracious. Charming. Encouraging. He treated me like a real princess. And his homilies, though painful at times, stuck."

"What was the first homily he taught you?"

"That's easy." For some reason she felt the sting of tears. "A Verdonian is born from the heart, not from the land."

"Ah." Brandt's voice turned gentle. "You must have been feeling out of place."

"Very much so. I'd just been told in no uncertain terms that I wasn't a 'real' princess. And more than anything I wanted to belong to the country I'd adopted as my own."

"He made quite an impression on you."

"Oh, he did. A lasting one. As did you." She narrowed her gaze on Brandt's face. "Now that I think about it, you two look a lot alike. He was gruff and craggy and those eyes—"

"Piercing."

"Again. Like yours." She cupped her chin, leaning her elbow on her knee. "Thank goodness he was there for you. It must have been difficult, losing your parents at such a young age."

"I don't have any real memories of them. They were killed when I was a baby." So calm. So accepting. "But I always had my grandfather. He taught me everything I needed to know."

"Let me guess. Honor. Duty. Responsibility. And…" She screwed up her face in thought. "And sacrifice. Am I close?"

"On the money. Though I might have said 'choice' rather than sacrifice, though it adds up to the same thing. The choices we're expected to make are for the good of the country rather than for our own betterment."

"And when the two are at odds?" she asked, curious.

"No contest," he answered promptly. "Verdonia wins every time."

She shook her head in exasperation. "You're so pragmatic."

He accepted the observation with a shrug and a slow smile. "And you're so…not."

She loved that smile. In fact, she'd worked hard over the past two weeks to win as many from him as she could. Considering how rare they were, she regarded them as more precious than gold. He continued to gaze at her for an endless moment. Something in those deep, dark eyes sent a shiver of awareness darting through her.

How old had she been when she'd first fallen in love with this man? Eleven? Twelve? Granted, it had been puppy love. But even then she'd been drawn to him, had been aware of him on some intuitive level. She'd almost forgotten those unbidden feelings, the sense that she'd finally found someone who fit her when she so clearly didn't fit in with the Montgomerys.

Tossing her damp hair over her shoulders, she

shifted so she could watch Brandt's expression while they talked. Nothing would make his face a thing of beauty. It was too hard, too austere, with eyes so grave and intent that most people had trouble meeting his gaze. Their intensity had never bothered Miri. She'd always been fascinated by them, and on some odd level, reassured. They were trustworthy eyes, eyes that didn't lie, no matter how tough the question or unpleasant the truth.

Right now, she wanted to hear the unvarnished truth. "I'm wondering what happens when we go home. Between us, I mean."

If her question threw him, he didn't show it. "What do you want to happen?"

"I want to continue the way we are now," she answered promptly, before correcting herself. "No. I take that back. I want more."

"More." He regarded her impassively for a long moment and then she saw a slow burn gathering in the ebony depths of his gaze, a burn that gave her hope. "Define more."

"Tell me something first. Is this just a fling we're having, or what?"

He settled back on his elbows, his features schooled to patience. "I don't think our relationship qualifies as a fling, no."

"Because we aren't sleeping together."

She scored another smile, this one wider than before. "You are blunt, aren't you?"

"It helps if you consider me refreshing. That's how my family describes me. Refreshingly honest." She linked her fingers together. "And you haven't answered my question. Are we having a fling?"

No equivocation. No hesitation. Just a simple "No."

"Oh." She cleared her throat. "Would you like to?"

He continued to lounge on the rock, resembling nothing more than a great sinewy panther. But underneath that casual manner, she could sense his gathering tension, as though he were ready to react to the least provocation. "What are you doing, Miri?"

"Don't you know? Can't you tell?" She was poking a big, dangerous cat with a stick. Brilliant.

"You're playing with fire," he warned, confirming her suspicions.

Not that his warning had much affect on her tongue. "I wouldn't mind seeing some of that fire," she informed him. "I sense it's there. Well hidden, but there someplace."

He moved with a speed and deadly intent that caught her by surprise. One second he lounged casually beside her, and the next he'd scooped her into his arms and flipped her onto her back. He leaned over her, his shoulders so wide they blocked out the sun.

"Shall I show you?"

CHAPTER FOUR

"I THINK this might be the 'something more' I had in mind."

"Might?" It took every ounce of Brandt's self-control to keep from taking her then and there. "I'd say it was definitely the 'something more' you had in mind. At least, it's the 'something more' *I* had in mind."

Miri stared up at him, her sea-green eyes soft and luminous. "Then why have you waited? Why haven't you tried to make love to me before this? Is it because of who I am?"

He wouldn't lie to her. "Yes. Who, what. There are warnings and conditions stamped all over you and I'd be a fool to ignore them."

"That's funny. I could have sworn the stamps had your name on them and maybe a small warning that says, 'Open with care.'"

"I wouldn't do it any other way." She was too precious for anything other than care. "Not with you."

He'd never been one to take advantage of a woman, and he didn't plan to start with Miri. All Brandt's previous lovers had known the score, he'd made certain of that. For the most part they'd been experienced women interested in a mature relationship. Since he refused to put an offer of marriage on the table, that's all he had to offer them. But with Miri, instinct warned him to tread carefully. She was a Montgomery. A Princess of Verdonia. He couldn't take a woman like this for his mistress, not without all hell breaking loose.

Miri's mouth curved to one side, a teasing look he'd become intimately familiar with. She loved to give him a hard time, and he found, much to his surprise, that he thoroughly enjoyed being on the receiving end of her ragging. "Tell me the truth. Do these warnings you claim to see scare you?" she asked, draping her arms around his neck.

"Without question."

"What if I gave you permission to ignore them?"

He released a frustrated bark of laughter. "I don't understand you. I never have."

Sooty brows drew together. "What's to understand?"

"Most people find me off-putting."

"Really?" Her eyes widened in mock innocence. "I hadn't noticed."

"That's the sort of thing I mean. They wouldn't have the nerve to tease me the way you do."

"And you've used that reaction to your advantage, haven't you?"

"It would be foolish not to." He cupped her face. "But it never worked with you. You were always perfectly comfortable around me. Why is that?"

"Because I know you. I recognize you. I did

from the first moment I saw you." Her arms tightened around his neck. "And I've learned something during our time here on Mazoné."

"I'm almost afraid to ask."

"I've realized how right this would be. Us. Together like this. Don't you feel it, too?"

He did. But it was too soon, with too much still unresolved between them. Once he took her, they'd be indelibly connected, joined in a way he didn't think she was prepared for. Theirs wouldn't be a casual fling, regardless of what she might think. He knew better. Taking this any further would bind them irrevocably.

Before he could set her aside, she lifted upward and sealed his mouth with hers. Her lips parted and she breeched inward for a delicious seduction, offering heat and passion and a burning desire. She left no doubt as to how much she wanted him. The sweet truth of it was there in her kiss, one that gave him every bit of herself, unrestrained, leaving herself open and vulnerable to rejection.

Not that he could reject her. He forked his fingers deep into the silken weight of her hair and deepened the kiss. A sigh of delight slipped from her mouth to his, a sigh that filled him with her essence, invaded every sense, over-riding sensibility. He could take her here and now, and she wouldn't offer a single word of protest. She'd submit. Hell, she'd more than submit. She'd welcome his possession.

"Miri, we need to stop." But even as he said the words, he slid his hand from her hair and followed the sweep of her neck to the edge of her bikini top. He traced the plunging line with a fingertip. "We can't let this go any further."

She shivered beneath the delicate caress. "Finish what you're doing and then we'll stop."

"Good plan."

He pinched the clasp between her breasts and a bubbling laugh escaped her. Peeling back the triangles of her top, he exposed her breasts. They were perfect, fitting into his palms as though made for his touch. The deep rose nipples tightened in reaction and he bent down to savor them. A musky woman's scent rose up to greet him. Her scent. A scent more erotic than any perfume.

He should stop. This was the wrong time, the wrong place, even if it was the right woman. If they took this the next step, he wanted a better understanding between them, to deal with the ramifications beforehand rather than with regret afterward.

"We can't." He shuddered with the need to finish what they'd started. "We can't do this now."

She peeked at him through lowered lashes. A delicate flush warmed the sweep of her cheekbones and gave a rosy glow to her breasts. "If not now, then when?"

He closed his eyes. "Tomorrow."

"Not tonight?" He could hear the disappointment in her voice.

"I have a business meeting. I don't know how late it'll run. And we need to talk before we take this any further." He looked at her then. "I'm not interested in something temporary. Not with you."

She smiled radiantly. "Neither am I."

Brandt drew a deep breath and refastened her top. Forcing himself upright, he held out his hand and pulled Miri to her feet. "Time to go."

He gathered her close and kissed her a final time. It was a kiss of longing. Of celebration. Of promise. Soon she would be his. And once she was, he'd have everything he'd ever wanted. Finally, he released her and she started to slip back into the pool. Brandt reached out and stopped her at the last minute.

"Tonight," he stated.

She didn't bother to ask what he meant. He could see in her eyes that she knew, her gaze promising a moon-drenched night filled with unforgettable passion. Or at least, he thought so, at that point.

By later that evening, King Stefan was dead

and Miri had returned to Verdonia. Of course, she left a note. But it was too late. By then, everything had changed. What had seemed so certain, would never be. His grandfather had taught him well. Honor. Duty. Responsibility. And one thing more. He thought he'd also learned choice at his grandfather's knee. But Miri had been right, after all.

What he'd learned was sacrifice.

Night had fallen on Brandt's wedding day hours earlier and the only light in the room came from a small fire blazing in the fireplace across from his chair, a fire he'd deliberately built for a single purpose. Opening the letter Miri had left for him on Mazoné, a letter creased from more readings than he could count, he traced the words written there. A bittersweet smile twisted his mouth as he reread it.

Miri's handwriting epitomized her perfectly—passionate and grief stricken. After explaining that she was on her way to the airport to fly home after learning of King Stefan's death, she'd then addressed her hopes for their relationship. Her feelings for him poured from every scrawled word, painting a beautiful, if impossible, future.

Once upon a time he thought he could have it all. A life with a woman who adored him, who wanted nothing more than to love him. To bear his children. To grow old with him.

He closed his eyes, picturing what would never be. He'd given himself these few hours to indulge in foolishness, something he couldn't afford to do again. This was his wedding day. Instead of marrying Miri Montgomery, as he'd once thought possible, he'd taken Alyssa Sutherland as his wife with a cold-blooded deliberation that he'd learned at his grandfather's knee. Well, he'd made his decision, and he wasn't a man for second thoughts or half measures. He'd committed himself to Alyssa and he'd live up to that commitment, no matter how difficult.

Up until now, he'd considered the Sutherland woman a nonentity. A tool. He drew in a deep breath. That would have to change now that she was his wife. He couldn't simply dismiss her from his mind and life because he would have preferred a different bride. She would be an integral part of his future and the future of Verdonia. As much as he resisted, she deserved answers. And soon, he'd offer them to her and see if they couldn't establish a marriage of compatibility and affection, if not love.

A hint of honeysuckle and coconut wafted upward in the quietest of protests. Not Miri's perfume. The sunscreen she'd worn on that last day by the waterfall. His smile faded with the memory. It was time. Time to bind himself to his wife. Time to move forward and never look back again. Leaning toward the fire, he allowed Miri's letter to slip from his hand. It floated in the air for a brief moment before swirling above the flames in the grate. The paper blackened and then the oils on it caught fire and in a soft whoosh it exploded in a shower of sparks. He waited until the last ember died, before closing his eyes.

"Goodbye, Miri," he whispered.

Miri froze in the private doorway between Brandt's suite and hers, watching as the letter she'd left for him in Mazoné drifted from his hand into the fire.

She covered her mouth with a hand to keep from crying out. He was breaking her heart, a heart she'd already thought broken beyond repair. Yet, seeing the undisguised despair lining Brandt's face she conceded that his decision to marry Alyssa hadn't come easily, and that he'd chosen this time alone to say goodbye to what they'd once shared.

Slowly, carefully, she drew in a deep breath. Then another. In the hours she'd been sitting in her room lost in memories, she'd reached a decision. She'd track him down and confront him. Demand an answer. But standing here, watching him, she realized he'd already given her that answer.

He'd married Alyssa—thought he'd married Alyssa—in order to win the throne. What more did she need to know? Not that his plan would work. Merrick would see to that. If Brandt became king, it would be in a fair election against Lander, not through an illicit marriage to Alyssa Sutherland.

It was pointless to stand here, expecting more from him, expecting something he couldn't give. She should leave now. Her job was done. She should return to Alyssa's suite and search the place for a paring knife or sewing shears and cut her way out of her wedding gown. Chances were she'd be able to slip away with no one the wiser.

But she didn't leave. Instead, she bowed her head and faced the painful truth. She didn't want to go. She wanted an opportunity to say goodbye, just as Brandt had. Looking up, she stared into the darkened room. The fire had died to a faint glow. The only other light came from a sliver of moon slipping in one of the windows to form a tight halo around the chair in which Brandt sat. Just one night, that was all she asked. One night to say farewell.

Not giving herself time to consider the foolishness of her actions, she entered the room. Silently, she crept across the carpet until she reached his chair. Once there, she crouched, staying well clear of the moonlight.

"Brandt," she whispered, doing her best to imitate Angela's accent, hoping she was correct in assuming it came close to matching Alyssa's.

His head jerked up and he glanced at her. A full minute ticked by before he spoke. "You surprise me, Princess."

"Why's that?"

"You're here. I thought I'd have to track you down."

She gave a careless shrug. "You might have, except for one thing."

"Which is?"

She allowed an exasperated note to enter her voice. "I can't get out of this stupid dress."

His features relaxed ever so slightly. "My apologies. I'd forgotten it would be necessary to cut you free. Another Verdonian tradition you may not be familiar with."

"Would you mind? It's getting late."

He stood, and so did she, her skirts rustling as she took a quick step backward, allowing the shadows to swallow her more fully. Bypassing her, he walked to a door leading to the outer corridor. Opening it, he spoke quietly to whomever stood outside. When he returned he held a dagger.

"Your men are well prepared," she commented faintly.

He shrugged. "It's part of their uniform," he said, reaching for a light switch.

"Don't." She fought to modulate her voice. "Please, I'd rather you didn't turn on the light."

"I need to see what I'm doing." She couldn't think of a reasonable response to that, but to her relief, she didn't have to come up with one. "But I won't turn it on if you'd rather I didn't. Let's see if this will work."

Returning to her side, he dropped a hand on her shoulder and guided her into the moonlight. She was careful to keep her back to him, terrified that he'd catch a glimpse of her face. Even though Merrick must have gotten far away by now, any extra time she could give him would only help. Not that her plans for this evening had anything to do with helping her stepbrother.

"Hold still," Brandt instructed, sweeping her hair off her back. "I don't want to cut you."

She felt a slight tug at her bodice before it loosened. Inch by inch it sagged forward, slipping from her shoulders. Folding her arms across her chest, she held the gown in place.

The silence grew deafening, broken only by the harshness of her own breathing.

When he finished cutting her free, he didn't step away. "Your skin is amazing." He traced a path from the nape of her neck to the base of her spine. "The moonlight has turned it to silver."

"What are you doing?" she whispered.

"You know what I'm doing." He continued his stroking touch, sending shivers shooting through her. "We can make this work, Alyssa."

Alyssa. Miri closed her eyes against the sharp bite of pain. "You really expect me to consummate this marriage?"

He continued to stand close, so tall he made her feel tiny. "Do you want romantic words? I can give them to you if you wish. But they wouldn't be true. Because the truth is, we need to consummate our marriage in order to make it legal." His hands tightened on her. "That doesn't mean it has to be an unpleasant experience or that we can't enjoy the physical part of our relationship. How we proceed from here is up to us. This can be a beginning, for both of us."

"You'd find it that easy?" It hurt unbearably to think so. "A tap to turn on or off? Is that how your emotions work?"

"No. No more than with you. But I'm determined to make our marriage work, if you're willing."

"We're strangers. You know nothing about me. And I—" Her hands clenched, her nails biting into her palms. "And I know nothing about you." She'd only thought she did. But she'd been wrong. So horribly wrong.

Sliding an arm around her waist, Brandt spooned her close, her spine tight against his chest. His hand splayed across her abdomen, warm and heavy and possessive. The warmth of his breath washed over her as he traced the curve between her neck and shoulder with his mouth. She shivered beneath the delicate caress, relaxing into his embrace. The instant she realized what she'd done, she stiffened in his grasp. Taking a hasty step forward, she edged farther into shadow.

He followed, maintaining contact. His fingers trailed along the path his mouth had followed, gently easing the gown off her shoulders. The sizzle from that stolen touch burned like fire, igniting a shockwave that caused the beadwork on her loosened gown to glitter in agitation.

"Slow and easy, wife," he attempted to soothe. "We have all night."

She'd thought she could do this, thought she'd steal this night with him with no one the wiser and no one hurt. But hearing him call her by another woman's name, having him address her as *wife* was killing her by inches.

"Maybe we should wait until tomorrow." The suggestion escaped in a breathless rush. "Wait until we've had a chance to get to know each other better."

"Nothing will have changed." He sounded so gentle, so caring. Almost tender. "Come tomorrow, we'll still be married. We'll still be relative strangers. And your apprehension will have another day to take root and grow."

"So we're better off getting it over with?"

"Better off discovering that you have nothing to fear."

"I'm not afraid," she instantly protested.

And she wasn't. She wanted to make love to Brandt. She just wanted him to know who he was loving, though she didn't dare reveal her identity. But perhaps…perhaps there was a way she could turn this around. If she could reach him on some level, if he recognized her—even subconsciously—maybe it would be enough. He'd still be responding to the uniqueness of her touch. To her personal scent and taste. To a kiss only she could give. In the end, he'd be making love to her, not to Alyssa, and she'd have to hope that some small part of him realized it.

Slowly, she lowered her arms, allowing her gown to slip downward. He accepted her silent surrender without comment. His touch remained gentle, careful. He eased the gown to her waist, then hooked his thumbs in both skirt and petticoats, and guided them down her hips. His palms swept the upper slopes of her buttocks, lingered, then moved on. Dropping to one knee, he helped her step free of the voluminous layers of silk.

Before she had time to feel self-conscious, he stood and turned her in his arms, taking her mouth with his. She remembered this kiss, had longed for it ever since that day by the waterfall. And she found herself returning it, tentatively at first, and then with mounting passion. His lips hardened, grew more forceful. But rather than protest, she met his demand with one of her own.

She barely felt the give of her bra, wouldn't have noticed if he hadn't feathered his fingertips from the sensitive sides of her breasts inward to the burgeoning tips. He stroked her with excruciating precision, as though he knew just where to touch in order to elicit the most intoxicating pleasure.

And just like that she realized what he was doing. He was seducing her, step-by-dispassionate-step. Moonlight slashed his face, revealing the remote determination in his eyes, as well as the calculation in his expression. And now that she understand what he was attempting she could feel it in his studied touch.

Miri shook her head. She didn't want him to make love to her, not like this, not with cold-blooded intent. Somehow she had to find a way to break through to the passion that lay beneath that carefully controlled exterior, like she had beside the waterfall.

"Wait," she whispered. She had to repeat herself before he broke off his siege. "Slow down."

She found his reluctance to release her encouraging, but it wasn't enough. She wanted an emotional bonding as much as a physical one. The moonlight had fled across the room and she shifted away from Brandt to follow it, standing so it cut across her from the nape of her neck to her calves. She could literally feel his gaze, like a line of fire tracing her spine. She drew a deep breath, aware that this next part would be the hardest thing she'd ever done.

With as much casual grace as she could muster, she removed first one glistening stocking, then the other, deliberately dipping and swaying as though to some private song. Next came her garter belt, a flimsy bit of silk in bridal white. And then all that remained was her thong. Gliding it down her hips, she gave a slow shimmy to send the scrap of lace floating to her ankles. Shaking her bleached hair back so it tumbled toward her hips, she half turned and glanced over shoulder.

From deep in the shadows she could hear the harsh give and take of his breath. Feel the want. Practically taste the desire that scented the air. Without a word, he ripped off his clothes with impressive haste. When the last piece of clothing hit the floor, he came for her, fast and determined, stepping from shadow to moonlight. And finally, finally, he allowed his emotions free rein.

His eyes heated, filled with an urgency she couldn't mistake. In response, her own body warmed with forbidden hunger. He paused when he reached her and touched a spot on her left hip. "What's this?"

Her breath caught. She'd forgotten all about that. "It's a tattoo." One she'd gotten after that memorable day by the waterfall.

"It's a butterfly."

"I like butterflies."

"I…I used to."

"Not anymore?" she dared to ask.

He shook his head, his mouth tightening. He ended the discussion by sweeping her up in his arms and carrying her to the bed. The sheets were cool against her back, a distinct contrast to the liquid heat coursing through her. Rolling onto his back, he lifted her on top of him.

His hold remained light, more embrace than grip. She wanted to wrap herself around him. Devour him. Drive every thought from his head but one.

Sinking downward, she covered the breadth of his chest with kisses. Her hair draped over and around them like the softest of cloaks and he shuddered in reaction. He reached for her, impatient, sliding her upward until she found his mouth again, and took it in quick, desperate kisses. It wasn't enough. Not nearly enough.

He must have felt the same. Flipping her onto her back, he levered himself above her. It was his turn to anoint her body, starting at the curve of her jawline and working downward. He lingered at her breasts, then skated to the curve of her belly before dipping lower, carefully avoiding her tattooed butterfly. He worshiped her with his mouth, finding and exploring the most sensitive spots on her body. By the time he'd finished, her body wept with a want more powerful than anything she'd ever experienced before.

She tried to say something, to plead. To beg for what she so urgently needed. He seemed to know already. Parting her legs, he slipped between them, then hesitated.

"I'll try not to hurt you."

Did he know? Had he picked up on her inexperience? He must have, for he eased his passage into her body and breached her innocence with exquisite care. Tears escaped from the corners of her eyes, dampening the hair at her temples. They weren't tears of pain, but tears of elation. If all she had was this one night with Brandt, she'd find a way for it to be enough. She whispered his name, her voice filled with wonder and joy.

He shuddered above her, shaking his head in disbelief. "It shouldn't be like this. I shouldn't feel like this." His throat worked. "But I do."

And then the ride turned wild, and they rode that wildness together in mindless ecstasy, burning painfully bright in the darkest part of the night. When the shattering came it went beyond all imagining, shaking Miri to the core. For endless minutes they clung to each other, lost to everything but the sensations that continued to shudder through them.

At long last, he rolled to one side and pulled her close, wrapping himself around her as though staking a claim. "I didn't think that was possible," he told her. "This changes everything. You know that, don't you?"

"Yes." She doubted she'd ever be the same again.

"Sleep," he urged. "We'll talk in the morning."

She didn't dare sleep. At some point, she needed to slip away. To leave and never look back. Snuggling deeper into his embrace she clung to each minute before it escaped her grasp, imprinted every second on her memory. The sound of his breathing and the gentle huskiness of his voice. The scent of his skin, as well as the perfume of their lovemaking. The final glow of moonlight as it kissed them farewell. The taste of his kisses that lingered on her lips.

Finally, she felt him relax into a deep sleep and cautiously untangled herself from his embrace. The worst moment came when she left the warmth of his bed. Tiptoeing across the room, she hesitated at the threshold connecting his suite with Alyssa's. Unable to resist, she glanced back.

As though aware of her regard, he stirred, groping for her. And then he said the one thing guaranteed to wound her more profoundly than anything else could have.

"Alyssa."

CHAPTER FIVE

Principality of Verdon, Verdonia
Ten weeks later...present time

"WE'RE going to get in trouble," Miri warned her two sisters-in-law. "As soon as my brothers realize we've given our security people the slip, they're going to hit the roof. I've seen it happen before and you don't want to be anywhere in the vicinity when they blow."

Lander's new bride, Juliana, gave her dark wig a final tug over deep red curls. "No worries. We won't be anywhere in the vicinity when they blow. We'll be at the mall."

She settled a pair of plain-lens eyeglasses on the tip of her nose, the amethysts on her wedding rings flashing like purple fire. As always, they drew Miri's gaze, particularly the new stone Lander had unearthed and named the Juliana Rose, an amethyst that was neither purple nor blue nor pink, but rather a unique combination of all three. It reminded her of something, something from her childhood. Though it had teased her for weeks now, she'd never quite been able to put her finger on what it was about the ring that troubled her.

"Just one hour without an entourage or body-guards or strangers watching my every move," Juliana was saying. Satisfied with her disguise, she turned to pose for the other two. "That's all I'm asking. Once Lander is elected king, I'll have a snowflake's chance in hell of ever being able to pull off something like this again."

"Lander will see to that." Miri could guarantee it. He'd proven himself intensely protective of Juliana, to the point of proposing to her just to salvage her reputation when the press had discovered they were lovers. And then he'd fallen in love with her. It had been a fairy tale come true. "You two have a lot to learn about my brothers if you think they won't have something to say about this little escapade."

"Stop being so pessimistic, Miri. I'm sure Merrick will understand." Alyssa made the statement with the blithe confidence of a brand-new bride blissfully in love with her husband and blind as a bat when it came to his flaws. Who'd have thought when Merrick had abducted her that they'd end up so happy together in such a short time? "We're all disguised. If anyone catches on or the press finds us, we'll leave. Where's the harm in that?"

"What if Br—Prince Brandt tries something again?" Miri fought back a blush at having stumbled over his name. "I'm familiar with the man's tactics. He doesn't give up easily. Look at what happened when he captured you and Merrick, Alyssa. There I was hiding on Mazoné, while you and Merrick were on the run, dodging Brandt's men. Then when you infiltrated his castle to rescue your mother, he sprung his trap. He was certain he'd married you. And when he realized he hadn't—"

"By kissing me!" Alyssa inserted indignantly.

"He then tricked you into revealing the true identity of his bride. Me." Miri broke off with a shrug. "As I said. Once Brandt is set on a path, he doesn't give up easily. If he's determined to win the throne, he'll find a way to get it."

Alyssa and Juliana exchanged worried glances, but it was clear they weren't concerned about Brandt's next move to gain the throne, so much as Miri's feelings for him. Obviously, they knew what had happened between the two after she'd taken Alyssa's place at the altar. She'd hoped she'd been successful at hiding her feelings for Brandt. Judging by their expressions, she'd failed miserably.

"He won't hurt you again," Alyssa reassured gently. "Merrick will make certain of it."

Tears welled into Miri's eyes, an all too common occurrence these days. "He didn't hurt me. Not the way you mean. I went to him, not the other way around."

Alyssa appeared shocked by Miri's confession, probably because Brandt terrified her. But Juliana's expression spoke of perfect understanding. These women had become so dear to Miri—the sisters she'd always longed for and never had.

"It's like that sometimes," Juliana stated with a knowledgeable nod. "If you'd asked me just a few months ago if I'd surrender common sense in order to be with a man, I'd have called you six different kinds of fool. Then I met Lander and the next thing I knew I'd lost every brain cell I possessed. Is that how it is with Brandt?"

"That's how it used to be." Miri shot to her feet, nearly unseating the light brown wig she'd been talked into donning. "The only feeling I have for him anymore is utter contempt. When he failed to steal the throne by marrying Alyssa, he reported Lander to the Temporary Governing Council and accused him of financial malfeasance. I'll never forgive Brandt for that."

"Maybe he believed your brother really was guilty." Alyssa's blue eyes widened as though astonished to find herself defending Brandt. She turned to Juliana for support. "Didn't you say that awful woman made it look like the Montgomerys were responsible for embezzling from Verdonia's amethyst mines?"

"Lauren DeVida." Juliana practically spat the name. "King Stefan's Chief Executive Accountant. More like his Chief Executive Thief, if you ask me. I hope they track that woman down and throw her in the deepest, darkest pit they can find."

A bit bloodthirsty, but considering Juliana had been the one to uncover the financial scam—a desperate and nearly impossible task that had taken every ounce of the financial wizard's mathematical skill and accounting genius—Miri could understand why she wanted to see Lauren DeVida suffer. And since it was

Juliana's frantic efforts to gather the necessary proof that had ultimately saved Lander, Miri could sympathize with her sister-in-law's desire for revenge.

"If we're going to go, we should get moving," Alyssa recommended. "Are you certain no one will notice the car's missing?"

Juliana shook her head. "Lander has a fleet of nondescript vehicles he uses whenever he wants to escape public scrutiny. I managed to get hold of one, but only until three o'clock."

"Four hours?" Alyssa released a sigh of delight. "I'll take it."

Instead of a wig, she'd opted for oversized sunglasses and a scarf to hide her distinctive blond hair, pairing them with faded jeans and a plain white blouse. If Miri hadn't known who Alyssa was, she'd never have suspected the truth. For the first time in weeks she felt a return of her old spirit. Why in the world had she tried to talk the other two out of this escapade when not so long ago she'd have been the main instigator?

"Okay, girls," she said, determined to shake the old Miri awake. "Disguises in place?"

Alyssa and Juliana both mugged in front of the mirror. "Set," they chorused.

"Keys?"

Juliana nodded. "I have it on excellent authority that they're under the floor mat in the car."

"Cell phones in case we get separated?"

"Check and double check."

Miri grinned. "And most important of all… credit cards?"

That led to a mad scramble to make sure they had adequate resources for their shopping trip. Once satisfied, they made their way from their rooms in the palace to where Juliana had arranged to pick up the car. They nearly gave themselves away any number of times as they made good their escape. It didn't help that after each close call, one of them would give a snort of laughter and the others would break down giggling.

When they finally reached the simple white sedan, they got into a brief disagreement over who would drive. Miri settled the issue by snatching up the keys. "I know the fastest way there and I'm used to Verdonian traffic. Now, do you want to spend what time we have at the mall, or arguing?" That simple question put an end to any further dispute and had them all piling into the car and on their way.

The next few hours proved a true pleasure. Miri loved spending time with her new "sisters," bonding over cosmetics, shoes and lattes. They lingered in the stores as long as they dared, delighted when their disguises proved a total success. It was Juliana who reluctantly brought the outing to an end.

"Okay, girls," she announced, snagging each by an arm. "I just got a call that Lander and Merrick have returned to the palace. We need to shake a leg before they realize we've gone missing."

Gathering up their packages, they made a beeline for the lowest level of the parking garage where they'd left the car. They were only a few spaces from it when a pair of SUVs shot toward them from different directions. Brakes squealed, reverberating through the cement structure. The two vehicles screeched to a stop so close that the three women crowded back against the rear door of a dusty minivan, completely boxed in.

"Merrick," Alyssa said with a groan. "This is what comes from marrying the head of Verdonia's Royal Security Force. Apparently his people out-covert your people, Juliana."

Before Miri could correct Alyssa's error, men erupted from the SUVs. But it was the one who took his time exiting that held her full attention and caused the breath to bottleneck in her throat. Anticipation vied with animosity, tying her stomach in knots. "It's Brandt."

He approached as though he had all the time in the world, sweeping them a courtly bow. "Your Highnesses." Apparently, their disguises didn't fool him for one little minute. After a single, all-encompassing look, his gaze settled on Miri. "It's time to come home, my dear. If you'll say goodbye to your in-laws, we can be on our way."

"Home?" Miri shook her head, incensed by his cavalier use of the word. After choosing another woman for his bride, after two and a half months of silence, he dared call Avernos her home? "No, thanks. My home is here."

"It *was* here," he corrected mildly. "You changed all that when you married me."

Was he kidding? "We're not married. That ceremony can't possibly be legal."

He lifted a shoulder in a careless shrug. "That's for the courts to determine. Until they say otherwise, you are my wife. And I intend to have my wife in my arms when I go to bed at night." He signaled to his men. "Ladies, if you'd please hand over your cell phones and car keys, I'd appreciate it."

Though phrased as a request, demand underscored every word. In response, Juliana's brown eyes glittered with fury while Alyssa appeared close to tears. Miri could have gone either way. Or managed both at the same time. So many emotions overwhelmed her she could barely think straight. Outrage and bitterness over how his decisions had destroyed their relationship vied with a stunned disbelief that he'd come for her after all this time. Worst of all a whisper of hope fluttered to life, small and fragile, like the wings of a butterfly.

After a momentary hesitation, her sisters-in-law complied with Brandt's directive. Juliana slapped her phone into the hand of the nearest man. "You won't get away with this," she told Brandt. "And don't think I won't find a way to make you pay for making me sound like I'm a B-rated movie actress in some schlock melodrama."

Alyssa tossed her cell phone toward Brandt before turning to give Miri a tight hug. "Don't be afraid," she whispered. "Merrick will find a way to rescue you. He's getting good at that sort of thing."

"You're mistaken, Princess," Brandt informed Alyssa. Based on his smile he'd overheard her comment and found it amusing. "My wife neither needs nor wants to be rescued. In fact, I suspect she's been waiting for me to show up."

"If you really believe that, you're delusional," Miri retorted.

Brandt's gaze grew painfully direct. "Not only do I believe it, so do you, whether you're willing to admit it in front of your sisters-in-law, or not. You're just hurt because I took so long coming after you. For that, I apologize."

She wanted to deny it, and yet, a small foolishly romantic part of her did feel a betraying bubble of elation. Or it did until her more pragmatic nature reacted with a healthy dose of suspicion. *Why* had he come? What new, more devious plan had he devised to thwart Lander and how did it involve her?

"You have a hell of a lot more to apologize for than this," she told him.

"No doubt you'll give me a detailed list. Now, as much as I'd like to discuss it further, we should be leaving. We're on a tight schedule. But first…" He snagged her wig and tugged it loose, watching in approval as her hair tumbled free. "Ah. Much better. And back to its natural color, I'm relieved to see."

She shook the heavy curtain from her face and debated her next move. Maybe if she could delay him a bit longer, Merrick really would come for them. "Since you brought it up, why have you waited so long to come after me?"

"I would have been here weeks ago, but you've been too well guarded until today."

Understanding dawned and she inhaled sharply. "Who's been reporting to you? Who told you about our plans today?"

"That's not important." He turned to address

two of his men. "We'll need half an hour to get to the landing site and take off. You will protect Princess Juliana and Princess Alyssa with your lives. In precisely thirty minutes, return the cell phones and have them call for assistance. You'll be notified when it's safe to leave them unattended. Do you have your exit plans in place?"

The two gave swift confirmations and took up a stance on either side of Juliana and Alyssa.

Brandt held out his hand to Miri. "Shall we go?"

He wasn't going to allow her to delay any longer. Ignoring his hand, she stalked toward the waiting SUV. She paused before climbing in and addressed her brothers' wives. "Tell Lander and Merrick not to do anything foolish, especially Merrick. I'll be in touch." She glared at Brandt. "You will allow me to call my family and reassure them that I'm safe and unharmed?"

He returned her cell phone to her. "Once

we're in Avernos, feel free to call them anytime you want. You're not a prisoner. Not exactly." He turned his attention to Alyssa. "Do thank Merrick for me, Your Highness. If he hadn't given me the idea, I'd never have thought to try this. But since abduction worked so well for him, I decided to follow his example. And he was right. It's an excellent plan."

"Right up until they arrest you and toss you into that pit my brothers have waiting for you," Miri shot back.

Brandt inclined his head with one of the slow smiles she adored—used to adore, she hastened to correct herself. "Yes," he concurred. "Right up until then."

Finally. Finally his wife was in Avernos where she belonged. Brandt leaned back in his chair and swirled his single malt, inhaling the peaty aroma. Miri may not want to stay, but he'd change her mind, no matter what it took. He swallowed deeply and dropped the glass to the wooden tabletop. He'd let her escape once. He wouldn't allow that to happen again.

The door opened and he stood, his gaze intent. Miri walked into his study, hell, stalked in, anger reverberating with every step. He silently scrutinized her, gauging her emotions. Furious, no doubt about that. But he could also see the hurt that underscored all else.

She wore a silk suit in blistering red. It was one of the outfits he'd personally selected in anticipation of her return, knowing she wouldn't have anything of her own with her. The tailored lines revealed the weight she'd lost, making her appear even more delicate than usual. She'd pulled her hair back from her face, inky dark once again, the heavy length gathered into a sleek knot at the nape of her neck. The style emphasized the fine-boned curves of her face and drew attention to her eyes, eyes the deep green of a stormy sea.

"It's good to have you here, Miri."

"I wish I could say the same. I've been in

touch with my family. Needless to say, they're not happy with you."

That had to be an understatement to end all understatements. "I'll deal with your family."

She approached, tossing her purse onto a side table before gesturing toward the chair in front of his desk. "Do you mind?"

He shook his head, amused. How could he have thought he'd ever be able to make a successful match with Alyssa? He wanted impulsive. Bold. Vibrant. A woman who brought color into his world. He wanted Miri. "Please, have a seat. I'm sorry I couldn't join you for dinner. Would you care for a drink?"

She shook her head. If he didn't know her so well, he'd think she were perfectly at ease. But he did know better. Her nervousness showed in the defiant slant of her chin and the tight grip she maintained on the padded arms of the chair. Even the curve of her mouth warned of emotional turmoil.

"Thank you for returning to Avernos," he began.

"Thank you for—" She stared in disbelief. "Have you lost your mind? You make it sound like I chose to return. In case you've overlooked a few dots, let me connect them for you. You gave me no other choice. I had to come back with you or you'd have—"

"I'd have…what?" he cut in.

She froze, like a deer scenting the approach of a predator. "Your men. You. You had all of us surrounded. I had to go with you."

"Do you think I'd have harmed you, or any of the Montgomery women for that matter?" He bit off each word, offended that she'd believe him capable of such a thing.

"Not harm, no," she conceded.

"You think I'd have forced you to come with me?"

Her head jerked up. "Yes." No equivocation this time, just that single fierce word.

He gave it a moment's consideration before

lifting a shoulder. She might be right. He sure as hell wouldn't have left without her, he knew that for a fact. "Perhaps I would have used force if there had been no other alternative. I don't know. But since you chose to come of your own free will, I didn't have to make that decision, did I?" He picked up his drink and drained it, before setting it aside. "Well? Shall we get down to it? Would you prefer to start, or shall I?"

"I'm not sure." She eyed his glass. "Are you sufficiently fortified?"

He couldn't help but smile. "There's no fortification sufficient enough when it comes to dealing with you."

She relaxed ever so slightly at the admission, but didn't respond to his smile. "You want to discuss our issues? Okay. I'll go first." She leaned forward in her chair, fixing him with an unforgiving stare. "The first thing we need to discuss is who betrayed me. I want to know who told you I'd be at the mall unescorted."

"Next question."

"Tell me who the traitor is," she insisted.

"I said, next question."

A silent battle of wills ensued, neither prepared to back down. He'd just begun to wonder if they were going to sit there all night when she released her breath in a frustrated sigh. "Fine. Don't tell me. Explain something else instead. What possible excuse can you have for what you've done? For the lengths you've gone to, to try and gain the throne?"

He wouldn't prevaricate over that question. She wanted the truth? He'd give it to her, no matter who got hurt. "I received evidence implicating the Montgomerys in the theft of Verdonia's amethysts."

Miri nodded impatiently. "Juliana discovered the person responsible. It was Lauren DeVida, my stepfather's Chief Executive Accountant. That's old news."

"It wasn't old when I received it."

She hesitated, frowning. "No, I guess it

wouldn't have been. But now you know the truth. That she was the one behind the thefts. That it wasn't the Montgomerys." Her voice gained intensity and he could hear the anger underscoring her words. "If you'd had the charges investigated when they'd first been given to you, you'd have discovered that for yourself. But instead, you used those accusations to try and snatch the throne from Lander."

He tilted his head to one side. Was she kidding? "How was I supposed to investigate the charges?" he demanded. "I didn't have access to the necessary records. I still don't. And I never will unless I'm elected king."

"Are you telling me you forced Alyssa to the altar in order to get your hands on a bunch of financial records?" she scoffed. "That's the excuse you're trying to sell?"

He fought the irritation that swept through him. "Sell? No. I'm telling you the unvarnished truth. Viable information was sent to me implicating your stepfather and Lander, and I considered any number of options before settling on marriage to Alyssa as my best option for resolving a critical situation. I had to protect Verdonia."

She waved that aside. "Oh, please."

He thrust a hand through his hair. Didn't she understand? "Listen to me, Miri. According to the experts I hired, the documents I received weren't faked. Someone has been siphoning off amethysts and selling them on the black market. And they've been doing it for a very long time. King Stefan was implicated directly, as well as Lander and Merrick, more recently."

"But it wasn't any of them," she argued. "I've explained that already. It was this DeVida woman."

He waited a beat before asking softly, "And who else?"

She looked taken aback. "Excuse me?"

"Think about it, Miri." Standing, he circled to the front of his desk, edging one hip on the tabletop directly across from her. "The amethysts leave the mines here in Avernos and are shipped to Celestia for processing. Some remain in Celestia and are purchased by local artisans, the rest go to Verdon for international sales and distribution."

"So?" she asked uneasily. "Every school-child knows that."

"My point is…how did Lauren DeVida steal the amethysts she sold on the black market?"

Miri stared at him blankly. "How did—"

"Lauren couldn't have done that on her own. It's not like she walked into the vault and helped herself to handfuls of uncut gems. There are only two places the amethysts could have been culled and the records altered." He ticked off on his fingers. "When they were brought out of the mines. Or when they were cut and graded in preparation for sale and distribution."

Miri fell silent, puzzling it out. "Whoever stole them wouldn't want uncut gems," she reluctantly offered. "They couldn't make as much from them."

"I agree. That suggests the second of our two possibilities is most likely. Which leaves us with the question of who. There's no way DeVida could have pulled this off on her own. She had to have help from someone, someone in a powerful position. Someone who could have circumvented the checks and balances King Stefan put in place. I want to know who that someone was."

"It wasn't my father!" Miri retorted, stung. "Or my brothers. We're not thieves."

"How do I know that?"

Hurt warred with anger. "How can you ask such a thing?"

"How can I not?" he asked grimly. "Look at it from my position. I receive incontrovertible evidence of a long-term theft ring that's brought Verdonia to a financial crisis. King Stefan was in charge during the years this was going on."

"He didn't know anything about it," she protested. "You can't blame him for that."

Brandt's expression hardened. "Yes, Miri, I can. It was his job to know. It was his responsibility. His duty as our king and protector." He hated criticizing the man she considered her father, but he had to make her understand it from his perspective. "His own accountant brought our country to the brink of ruin. And Stefan didn't have a clue. Why would I trust Lander to do a better job? Why should Verdonia?"

He winced at her drawn expression. "So you forced Alyssa to the altar because you didn't trust Lander? Is that what you're telling me?"

"My goal was to prevent any further malfeasance and to ensure that something like this never happens again. It's my duty to protect the people of Verdonia. To safeguard their future. The only way I can do that is from the throne. You may not approve of my methods, but at the time I didn't see any other option. Looking back, I still don't."

She stiffened. "My God," she whispered in disbelief. "You'd do it again, wouldn't you?"

"Marry Alyssa in order to keep Lander off the throne?" He didn't even hesitate. "Yes, I would."

"Regardless of what happened between us on Mazoné? Regardless of what we had?"

"Damn it, Miri." He scrubbed his face with his hands. "Do you think that doesn't tear me up? That I wouldn't wish for a different life, if it were possible? But, it's not. I am who I am. I can only act the way I've been raised to behave. The way I'm ethically bound to respond. I can't change that."

"Ethically bound?" She jumped to her feet and shot away from him. Halfway across the room, she spun around again, a flame of red fire. "Alyssa didn't want to marry you, Brandt. She was terrified, both of you and the situation she found herself in. But that didn't matter to you, did it? You sacrificed her on the altar of your precious code of ethics. She was no more than a pawn to you. How can that be right? How can that be just?"

He didn't back away from the question, but faced it squarely. "Not a day goes by that I don't regret what I did to her and to Angela." Pain carved deep crevices in his face. "It came down to forcing her to marry me and saving Verdonia, or allowing the corruption to continue until the entire country was destroyed. What should I have done?"

"That's so obvious, even a child could answer." Scorn filled her voice. "You should have brought the matter before the Temporary Governing Council, as you ultimately did."

He conceded the point with a nod. "Perhaps. But I couldn't be certain how deep the corruption ran. At the time, I didn't feel I could take the risk. Only after my initial plan failed did I dare take that route."

"So marrying Alyssa seemed like the best option, despite what we'd shared in Mazoné." She didn't phrase it as a question.

"The only option," he confirmed.

"Then what am I doing here? You brought me back to Avernos." Her hands fisted at her sides. "Why?"

A muscle jerked in his jaw. "You're here because I can't let you go." The words held a raspy edge. "I won't."

"And I won't be a consolation prize. Nor will I be second choice." She marched across the room and snatched up her purse. "You don't have the right to keep me here any longer. I want to go home. And by home I mean Verdon. Do you take me, or do I place another call to my brothers?"

Surging to his feet, Brandt came for her. "There's only one place you're going and it sure as hell isn't Verdon." Before she had time to react, he scooped her up in his arms and carried her toward the door.

"Let me go!" She fought to free herself, not that it did any good. "What do you think you're doing?"

"Taking you to my bed," he answered promptly. "Maybe once I have you there again you'll remember why you stayed the last time."

CHAPTER SIX

MIRI struggled in Brandt's arms, not that it did a bit of good. He carried her easily. To her outrage, the guards and servants littering the hallways were quick to avert eyes and hide smiles. How could they find this amusing? He was abducting her, holding her against her will!

Shoving open the door to his suite of rooms, he dropped her to her feet. "I'm not staying here," she informed him, backing away.

"You can try to leave, but you won't get far." He pursued her, his face set in inexorable lines. "Not again. My people won't make the same mistake twice."

"Don't blame them. It wasn't their fault," fairness compelled her to say. She edged her way clear across the room. Bumping up against the chair by the fireplace, the back of her knees clipped the seat and she sat down hard. Her cheeks turned a shade darker than her suit, but she recovered with impressive speed. Acting as though she'd planned to sit all along, she crossed her legs and smoothed the narrow skirt of her suit over her thighs. "They were ordered to guard Alyssa Sutherland, not Miri Montgomery. I made it clear who I was when I left. Why would they stop me?"

He took up a position in front of the mantel, far too close for comfort. "And because of that, you waltzed right out the front door."

"More of a stumbling run than a waltz," she muttered. Stiffening her spine, she fought to regain her focus and deal with the panther she somehow found herself caged with. Years of practice handling awkward situations in the course of performing her royal duties came to her rescue. "Let's have it, Brandt. What am I doing here?"

He regarded her in thoughtful silence for a

brief moment. She'd never seen eyes such a rich ebony, nor so piercing in their intensity. Thunder rumbled in the distance, a perfect punctuation to his stare. "There are any number of issues we need to address. But why don't we start with a certain wedding ceremony that took place a couple months ago."

"Oh. That." She managed to dismiss its importance with a blithe carelessness. And if she took pleasure in the fact that his mouth compressed in annoyance, well, who could blame her? "I don't suppose you have any idea whether or not we're really married?"

"No, I don't."

She grimaced. He'd managed to out-blithe her and with irritating ease, too. "You haven't checked?"

"I'm satisfied with the status quo."

That had her mouth falling open. "You must be joking."

"Not at all." He folded his arms across his chest. "As far as I'm concerned we're married."

She uncrossed her legs, her heels hitting the floor with a decisive thud. "You can't possibly believe our marriage is legal. It can't be." She ticked off on her fingers. "You married me thinking I was Alyssa Sutherland. Her name was the one used during the ceremony, and on all the paperwork. Any one of those facts must be grounds for an annulment."

"Quite possibly." He tilted his head to one side. "What do you suppose would happen if I claim I knew it was you all along?"

She shook her head, alarmed. "That's impossible. You didn't know. You couldn't have!"

"You're certain of that?"

He'd left her grappling for a response. "If you'd known, you'd have stopped the ceremony. You'd have ordered your men to find Alyssa, just as you did later that night."

"Actually, it was early the next morning, not that it matters. Now, pay attention, wife." He leaned forward, crowding her to the point that she inched back in the chair. Lightning flashed, followed by a sharp crack of thunder as the storm closed in. She swallowed convulsively, her pulse fluttering in the hollow of her throat. "Since you're responsible for me losing my bride, I've decided you can replace her. Maybe our wedding ceremony is legal. Maybe it's not. To be honest, I don't give a damn either way because I plan to fight the dissolution. So prepare yourself, my sweet. If you want out of this marriage, you have an uphill battle ahead of you."

She shot to her feet. It helped that she'd found a pair of sky-high heels among the clothes he'd purchased for her. The extra height gave her a feeling of parity, even if an artificial one. "You can't fool me a second time. I know why you're doing this."

"Interesting. And why is that?"

"You're hoping that marriage to me will give you some of the votes you may have lost when Alyssa married Merrick." Her accusation had him staring in patent disbelief. "Well, it won't work. I—"

He held up a hand to halt her tumble of words. "Let me get this straight. I'm using you for votes. You're saying that with a straight face?"

She gave a decisive nod. "Yes. And it won't work." She planted her hands on her hips. "Not only won't *I* vote for you, I'm going to actively campaign for Lander."

He began shaking his head before she'd even finished speaking. "Campaigning for your brother might prove difficult."

His voice had gone deadly quiet, a warning sign if she'd ever heard one. Not that she'd allow it to intimidate her. Her chin shot up and she steeled herself for the coming confrontation. "And why is that?"

He straightened from his lounging position against the mantel. "Pay attention, wife." He used the word deliberately as he took a step toward her. "You're here of your own choice. But it's my choice when you leave."

She fell back a pace. This time instead of falling into the chair, she circled behind it, desperate for the barrier it provided. Rain stung the windows and another flash of lightning bled the room of color. Gripping the upholstered chair back, she confronted him. "Choice? You didn't give me a choice about coming here and you darn well know it. And now you think you can keep me here? Against my will?"

"Yes and yes."

That took the wind out of her sails. "Has it occurred to you that holding women against their will is becoming a bad habit of yours?"

He pretended to consider. "You know, you could be right. I'll take your concerns under advisement."

His levity left her quivering with the need to hit out. "Fair warning, Your Highness. I'm not staying. I came with you today for one reason and one reason only. To—"

"Rub my nose in how you helped Merrick steal my bride?" he offered helpfully.

"Yes. No!" She thrust a hand through her hair, loosening the knot. "Okay, maybe."

A brief smile came and went. "Admit it, Miri." His voice took on a more serious tone. "You came with me because you're furious. And hurt. You want to share the pain."

"You think I'm that petty?" She glared at him for endless seconds before her face crumpled and she slammed her fist into the upholstered chair back. "Damn you! You're right. I am that petty. I want you to hurt as much as I've been hurt. I want you to suffer for what you did to our relationship. But most of all, I want you to know that I despise you for what you've done, for being such an unbelievable bastard."

He came for her, reaching for her even when she threw up her hands to ward him off. Pulling her into his arms, he simply held her. It didn't seem to matter how rigidly she stood, he wouldn't be put off. He smoothed back her hair and the loosened coil unraveled beneath his touch.

"How could I have ever thought this belonged to Alyssa?" he murmured, filling his hands with the weight of it. "Or that it wasn't you I held in my arms. Maybe I did know on some unconscious level, knew and ignored the signs because desire overrode common sense."

"You didn't know it was me." Could he hear the hurt? Did he even care? "You called me by her name."

"Of course I did. You were using her name." His eyes narrowed and her heart skittered in her chest at his sudden look of comprehension. Thunder crashed overhead and echoed off the surrounding mountains. "My God. Were you hoping I'd figure it out? Is that why you're so offended?"

Yes, yes and yes! How could he be so blind? "You should have realized who I was the moment you kissed me," she said, horrifying herself by the accusation. Pain ate through her at the memory and her hands fisted around the lapels of his suit jacket. "Is my kiss so common, so ordinary, that you couldn't tell it from another woman's?"

"Do you think if it had really been Alyssa I held in my arms that I would have reacted the way I did with you?" he countered. "Lost control the way I did? I may not have been consciously aware it was you I took to my bed, but on some level I knew."

"How can you say that? In your head, in your heart, you made love to Alyssa, not to me." It took every particle of restraint to speak the words, instead of howl them every bit as fiercely as the storm lashing at the windows. "You never gave me a single thought."

"You're wrong." His face darkened, filled with all the passion she could have wished. His eyes burned with it. His voice hungered from it. She could practically inhale the scent of it, a blatant need that electrified the very air they breathed. "The woman in my arms, the woman in my bed, the woman who caused me to lose every vestige of control was you. No other. And no other woman could have had the affect on me that you did."

"I don't believe you. I won't." She struggled to free herself, but he simply held on, refusing to release her. "Let me go!"

"Easy, sweetheart. Take it easy," he soothed.

She'd already discovered how pointless it was to struggle against him. That didn't mean she'd yield. She could still fight, with words, if nothing else. "Don't you dare call me sweetheart," she bit out. "You have no business keeping me here. No business touching me. No business forcing me to stay with you. You lost that privilege when you decided to marry Alyssa."

"I disagree. When you took her place, you gave me the right to keep you." He swept his thumb across her mouth. "To touch you."

"I never—"

"You did, Miri." His voice held an implacability she couldn't miss. "And you'll stay with me for as long as it takes."

"As long as what takes?" she demanded unevenly.

He cupped her face, turning it up to his. "For me to convince you that you belong here," he stunned her by saying. Lightning flickered, throwing his face into a stark relief that underscored his resolve. "You made promises to me and I intend to hold you to them."

"You must be kidding!"

"Not even a little. I might not have figured out who you were during the ceremony. And I may not have fully sensed the truth afterward. But you were well aware of who you promised to love, honor and cherish."

"I had to make those promises," she protested. Did he catch the defensive edge in her voice? Probably. Brandt didn't miss much. "If I hadn't repeated the vows, you'd have known I wasn't Alyssa."

He shook his head. "Not good enough. I heard your voice. I heard the emotion that permeated every single word. At the time, I thought you were pretending for our guests. But that wasn't true, was it?"

"I played a part. I was an actress performing a role, no more," she instantly denied. Who was she trying to convince, herself or Brandt? "I did what I had to in order to give Merrick and Alyssa time to escape. I'd have done anything to stop you, to keep you from stealing the throne from Lander."

"If that's true, then why did you stay?"

Naturally, he'd found the one flaw in her argument and nailed her with it. He studied her with an all-too-familiar mask, an inscrutable one that in the past had always filled her with intense frustration. How did he manage to keep his emotions in such an iron grip, when hers leaked from her grasp like a handful of water? He'd become a master at throwing up walls, walls she'd only managed to fully breach once before—on their wedding night.

"You had plenty of time to leave before night

fell, yet you didn't," he continued when she remained silent. "Why?"

Her chin shot up. No way would she humiliate herself with the truth. "As I said, I stayed to give Merrick as much time as possible to get away." She offered the lie without a moment's compunction.

His eyes were jet-black and so direct it was everything she could do not to flinch. "You made love to me, sacrificed your virginity, for the sake of kin and country?" he demanded. "Is that what you're trying to sell me?"

She opened her mouth to agree, but the words died unuttered. "Okay, I didn't stay with you to save Verdonia," she said with a sigh.

To her surprise, he relaxed ever so slightly. "Good answer."

"Would you have believed me if I'd insisted that it was the real reason?" she asked, curious. "Would you have believed me capable of making love to you as part of Alyssa's abduction plan?"

"No." Swift and unequivocal and punctuated by a hard rumble of thunder. "There's only one reason you'd ever go to bed with a man."

She fixed her attention on the tie knotted at his throat. It was slightly askew and for some reason that tiny imperfection filled her with a painful longing. She wanted to reach up and straighten that tie, to be entitled to perform such a casual, wifely duty. But she wasn't. He'd chosen to give another woman that right. "If you already know why I'd sleep with a man, then you don't need an answer from me."

"I want to hear you say it anyway." A quiet urgency reverberated through his statement. "I want to hear you say you'd only give yourself to a man because you loved him."

She shook her head, unwilling to hand him such a huge portion of her soul. "I didn't stay because I loved you. I just wanted to say good-bye." It took every scrap of poise she possessed to look him straight in the eye and make truth from fabrication. "I said everything I needed to that night. I've worked through any lingering feelings I might have had for you. Whatever was between us has died a painful death, and I have no interest whatsoever in trying to resurrect it."

"I don't believe you."

She ripped loose of his embrace and finally he let her go. No sooner did she gain her freedom, than she found herself longing to be back in his arms again. "Believe what you want, Brandt. It doesn't change anything. I came here to confront you over what you've done and to tell you how despicable I think you are."

"And that's the only reason?"

"No." She'd recovered a modicum of her composure. Tossing back a swathe of hair, she faced him with a determined expression. "I also came with you today in order to find out what you plan to do next."

"Next?"

"To steal the election from Lander. Fair warning, I won't let you try anything else that might harm him or my family."

Anger flashed like lightning. "How are you planning to stop me?"

"Any way I can."

Where before his smile warmed, this time it chilled. "Then I suggest you stay close and watch carefully."

"Trust me, I will."

"Fine. Let's start here and now."

Brandt stripped off his suit jacket, and then his tie, and tossed them in the direction of the chair. His shirt followed a moment later. He watched as Miri fought to keep her attention on his face. But she betrayed herself with fleeting looks that swept across his bared chest and arms. They were hungry little glances, filled with the memory of another time and another night. Glances that gave lie to her claims of indifference. Glances that burned as much as if she'd branded him with an actual touch.

"What do you think you're doing?" she asked faintly.

"I'm turning in for the night. Why?"

Her head jerked toward the bed and away again. A hint of color bloomed across her cheekbones while memories darkened her eyes to the green of a forest buried in shadow. "In that case, I'll turn in, too." She hovered in the center of the room, appearing momentarily helpless. "Where do I…"

He gestured toward the bed. "Right there. Next to me."

He fought to hide his amusement at the way her mouth opened and closed. And those amazing eyes of hers went so wide he could have drowned in them.

"You must be joking."

"I told you in the parking garage. I intend to have my wife in my arms when I go to bed." He crossed to her side and snagged the lapel of her suit, anchoring her in place. Not giving her time to react, he plucked open the first button of her jacket. "Starting now."

"Stop it, Brandt." The breath trembled from her lungs and she attempted to refasten the buttons as fast as he unfastened them. "This isn't funny."

"I agree." He won the battle of the buttons and slid the jacket off her shoulders, allowing it to drop to the floor at her feet. "There's nothing in the least amusing about our relationship to date."

She slapped at him as he tackled the zip of her skirt, not that it did any good. "I'm not sleeping with you," she wailed.

"Fair enough. Then you can lie awake in my arms while I sleep." His hands closed around her waist and he lifted her. Her skirt plummeted down her hips, catching momentarily on the toes of her mile-high heels before both shoes and skirt gave up the fight and dropped to the floor.

"You have no right," she protested as he set her down.

"I repeat. You gave me that right." He yanked her silk shell up and over her head.

"We can't. Our marriage isn't legal." The words were muffled, but he caught the gist.

"It is until we're told otherwise."

She emerged from beneath the shell, hair tousled, face stormy. "I don't want to go to bed with you."

"I got that message." Loud and clear. "Want or not, like or not, you will join me in that bed."

He spoke in a voice rare for him, but one that guaranteed instant obedience the few times he used it. She stood before him in scraps of lace and silk, rumpled and ruffled, and still defiance vibrated in every muscle of her body. Tears glistened, most likely from anger, though it could be distress, and he steeled himself to ignore their impact. He didn't dare show any weakness with her, not until matters were resolved between them.

He approached and she stumbled backward a step before locking her knees in place and holding her ground with clenched fists and a jutting jaw. So strong, so defiant, so painfully defenseless. Reaching past her, he flipped off the light.

"We're both tired and irritable and this isn't the best conversation to hold when we're not at our best," he spoke into the dark. "I suggest we table it until morning."

He heard her breath escape in a relieved rush. "I can live with that."

"Fine. Then I have something for you."

He crossed to his dresser, moving through the unlit room with complete assurance. Opening the top drawer, he grabbed one of the nightgowns he'd purchased with her in mind. He'd gone a little crazy, buying a full dozen, each softer and more filmy than the one before, some silk and some the finest cotton he could find, but all barely enough material to fill his palm.

"Here, put this on." He tossed her the first one that came to hand. Even in the dark, the light color of the gown made it visible. It billowed as it floated in her direction, and she snatched it out of midair before retreating deeper into shadow.

He could hear the rustle of clothing as she stripped and struggled not to think about what she was doing or how she looked doing it. That path led to trouble. If he were going to get through the endless hours ahead with his sanity intact, he'd better keep his thoughts on something other than Miri undressing, Miri naked, or Miri undressing and naked.

He'd almost succeeded when a flash of lightning lit the room for a split second, spotlighting his wife and forever burning a picture of her nudity into his heart and mind. The sight sent a kick straight to the gut, robbing him of the ability to breathe.

She stood, tautly erect, arched slightly backward as she lifted the nightgown above her head. Her breasts were full and beautifully rounded, tipped in rose, while a river of ebony hair cascaded down her shoulders and back, just brushing the curves of a perfectly curved backside. Her legs were glorious, toned and shapely, and she'd turned just enough toward him to reveal the thatch of dark curls that stood out in stark relief beneath the unblemished ivory of her belly.

He saw it. He saw it all in that brief instant before the room was plunged into darkness once again. And seeing, he wanted. He wanted to snatch her from where she stood and rip the nightgown from her grasp. More, he wanted to carry her to the bed and brand every lush inch with his possession. Desire raged, the need that screamed through him so intense he thought he'd lose his mind from the over-whelming demand of it. Only one thing held him in place—the expression in her eyes, an expression of utter vulnerability.

"Please," she whispered into the night.

Her voice echoed that vulnerability with an apprehension so sharp, it cut like a knife. He'd already hurt her, hurt her more than any man had a right to. He wouldn't add to that pain.

"It's okay, Miri." His voice sounded like it was filled with grit, but at least it held steady and gave a semblance of calm. With luck, it wouldn't frighten her. He deliberately kept his distance, determined to ease her trepidation. "Come to bed."

"I—I don't feel well."

He could read between those lines. "It's been one of those days," he told her gently. "You'll feel better once you've had some sleep."

"I'd rather sleep alone."

"I'm sure you would. And I wish I could let you." He closed his eyes for an instant, his hands fisting at his side. "But I'm not that altruistic."

Lightning cut through the room again, punctuated by a rumble of thunder. She'd finished changing and the staccato flash darted through the fine cotton of her nightgown, showing him all he dared not touch. The strobe of light also sent her flying across the room, but not toward the bed. She slammed into the bathroom and an instant later he heard her retching.

He came after her at a run. "Easy, sweetheart." Sinking to his knees behind her, he held her hair back from her face. "It's going to be okay. I've got you."

When she was done, she collapsed against the wall, drawing her knees tight against her chest. Tears leaked from behind her tightly closed eyes, tracking down cheeks bleached bone-white. If he'd thought she'd looked vulnerable before, it was nothing compared to how she looked now.

He settled down beside her and to his relief, she turned to him, huddling in his arms. And then she fell apart. He held her close and waited out the storm. When it had passed, he caught her hand in his and laced their fingers

together. There was only one reasonable question to ask.

"You're pregnant, aren't you?"

CHAPTER SEVEN

MIRI pulled back and stared at Brandt in horror. "No. No, that's not possible."

He swept her hair from her damp face. "It's quite possible. We made love two and a half months ago without protection." He lifted an eyebrow. "Were you on the pill at the time?"

Catching her bottom lip between her teeth, she shook her head. "No."

"And since we made love?" he pressed. "Has there been any indication you might *not* be pregnant?"

"I…I can't remember." What a liar she was. She knew full well she hadn't had a period since that amazing night. But that didn't mean she was pregnant. Desperation goaded her to debate the issue. "I've always been irregular.

Stress can cause that sort of reaction. And so can the recent weight I've lost."

"As can pregnancy, or so the rumor goes."

"Oh, very funny." The tenderness with which he regarded her had tears flooding her eyes again. "I'm not pregnant. I can't be."

"It's a far more likely cause than either stress or weight loss." Leaving her side, he rose long enough to dampen a washcloth with warm water before joining her on the floor again. "Damn, Miri. Don't cry," he murmured as he rinsed her face. "It'll all work out."

"There's nothing to work out," she argued tearfully around the washcloth. "You have your life and I have mine. Problem solved."

He continued as if she hadn't spoken. "It's too late to do anything about this tonight. I'll call the doctor first thing in the morning and have him fit you in for an exam. I promise, he'll be discreet."

That dried her eyes. She pulled away from Brandt and stood, annoyed to find her legs weren't as steady as she'd have liked. "Don't interfere in this, Your Highness. I'll make my own doctor's appointment."

He gained his feet, as well. "As soon as possible, please."

Did he think her a complete idiot? "I wouldn't do anything to jeopardize the baby's health—assuming there is a baby." Her hand stole downward, splaying across her abdomen. Did a child rest there? A child Brandt had given her? His eyes narrowed at the telling gesture. "Of course, I'll see a doctor as soon as possible."

"Why haven't you before this?"

It was an excellent question. She opened her mouth to tell Brandt it was none of his business, but one look at his face convinced her of the wisdom of a candid reply. "I went back to Mazoné after…after Alyssa's abduction," she admitted reluctantly.

"Staying clear of the line of fire?"

"It seemed a smart choice," she muttered.

"A very smart choice." An odd expression

glittered in his eyes, something hard and predatory that mingled with a lingering anger. "I'm not sure we'd have dealt well together those first few days after I found out the true identity of my bride."

Miri froze beneath that look. Brandt had always kept his emotions under tight control. Observing him now, she realized that control had evaporated when he'd learned of her identity. What would he have done if she'd been closer at hand? She shivered. Probably best she didn't know, and even better that she hadn't found out at the time.

"I stayed on Mazoné until right before Lander's wedding." They'd been long, hideous days of endless regret. But if the days had been bad, the nights had proven worse, plodding by, each interminable hour filled with a painful yearning. "To be honest, I lost track of time. I'd just begun to suspect something was out of kilter when I returned to Verdonia."

He nodded in perfect understanding. "I'm

guessing it would have raised a few eyebrows if you'd run out to the corner druggist and picked up a pregnancy test."

"Something like that." More like it would have swept across Mt. Roche within the hour. And then all hell would have really broken loose.

He handed her a toothbrush loaded with toothpaste and waited until her mouth was full of foam before continuing. "I know you don't want me interfering. But if you're pregnant, it's with my baby. Just so we're clear about this, I plan to involve myself in every aspect of the birth and rearing of our child."

She rinsed her mouth before turning to confront him. "You only suspected I was pregnant two minutes ago and you're already planning the delivery and parenting of our baby?" She lifted an eyebrow, struggling to present a strong front when all she wanted to do was pull the covers over her head and cry herself to sleep. "You can't even be certain it's yours."

He didn't hesitate. "If you're pregnant, it's mine."

Exhaustion stole the fight from her. "Fine. It's yours. Now, back off, Brandt. You're crowding me."

He ignored her, sweeping her into his arms. "I'll back off once I'm sure you're able to stand without help."

Unable to resist, she dropped her head to his shoulder. "I just need some sleep."

"I'll make sure you get it."

He lowered her to the bed and she turned her back on him, curling into a tight ball. Padding across the room, he opened the windows and an instant later a soft breeze swept through the room, carrying with it a rain-swept freshness. He returned to the bedside and she caught the rustle of his clothing as he stripped, before the mattress depressed beneath his weight. An instant later he wrapped her in the warmth of his arms.

"Close your eyes, love. We'll deal with all this tomorrow."

"I think I'd be more comfortable sleeping in my own bed," she whispered. "I can't do this. Here. With you."

"You don't have to do anything, sweetheart. Just sleep."

"You won't… You aren't—"

"I won't. I'm not. Not until you're ready."

"Thank you."

He didn't answer, just spooned her more tightly against his chest and she realized she'd been wrong. Horribly wrong. She wouldn't be more comfortable sleeping in her own bed. Having him with her, holding her again, was a pleasure just this side of heaven.

Sleep had just started to lay claim when she felt his hand shift, his fingers spreading wide and low across her belly. Her breath escaped in a trembling sigh. "I may not be pregnant," she murmured.

"But if you are…" His hand warmed her

through the thin cotton of her nightgown. "Our baby sleeps here," he marveled. "A son or a daughter."

"Or twins. Fraternal twins run down my mother's side."

He laughed and she could feel the rumble reverberate down the length of her spine. "Heaven help us if they're as impulsive as you."

She could picture it, picture it as clearly as though her children stood before her. A daughter with her father's dark hair and eyes and serious nature, calm and logical and brilliant. And a son whose mischievous eyes were the same green as her own, who caused his parents fits with the trouble he seemed to generate as easily as breathing.

Her eyes squeezed closed. If she listened hard enough, she could almost hear them. Their laughter. Their sweet voices calling to her. Their unique scent when she enfolded them in her arms. She wanted that. She wanted those babies more than she'd ever wanted anything in her life—with one exception.

Brandt. It wouldn't be the same without him. Her life would be full, but missing the most important ingredient if he weren't at her side. It didn't matter what had come before, did it? Not if they worked together to create a new life. They had a chance, right now, if they could only put the past behind them and move forward.

She slipped her hand on top of his, lacing their fingers together across their future. "What will we do if I am pregnant?"

"What we're doing now. We'll create a life for ourselves."

It was almost a mirror image of her own thoughts and she smiled. "And if our marriage is annulled?"

"If that happens, I plan to drag you in front of the nearest official and have us wed within the hour."

"And if I refuse?"

"You won't refuse. You wouldn't do that to our children." His hand tightened on hers. "You wouldn't do that to us."

"A baby isn't going to solve our differences. Nor will marriage."

"No. There's only one thing that will do that, and that's time for us to work things out." He feathered a kiss across the top of her head. "Sleep now, sweetheart. You need your rest. Everything else can wait until the morning."

Miri closed her eyes and allowed sleep to claim her. And as she drifted off her last thought was one that put a smile on her mouth. Morning. When morning came she'd be where she most wanted—safe in Brandt's arms.

Brandt hung up the phone and swore beneath his breath. Shoving open the doors that led onto the private balcony off his study, he crossed to the balustrade and folded his arms across the top railing. He drew in a deep breath, struggling to regain his control. The mountains were alive with birdsong and a soft, cool wind swept down the hillside, filled with the scent of cedar and wild grass. Nature at its best and yet it did nothing to soothe his temper.

"Brandt?" Miri joined him on the balcony. "I've been looking everywhere for you." She broke off, instantly picking up on his fury. Crossing to his side, she gripped his arm. "What's wrong? What's happened?"

"I've just been informed that our marriage has been invalidated."

A slight frown touched her brow, but she shrugged it off. "We expected that."

"True." His mouth twisted to one side. "Just not so soon. I'd hoped to have more time. But apparently your family isn't interested in giving us that time."

"They're involved in the dissolution?" she asked, shocked.

"Lander called, personally. He's instructed me—" Brandt released a harsh laugh. "Hell, why be diplomatic? He ordered me. He's ordered me to return you within twenty-four hours or he'll make the abduction public knowledge. He'll also be—and I quote—obligated to act. No doubt Merrick's security force is planning the takedown as we speak."

"I came to tell you my doctor's appointment is tomorrow. Once we announce I'm pregnant, they won't interfere if we choose to remarry." She hesitated, seeming to force out the words. "Unless…unless you'd rather end our relationship. If it's become a roadblock—"

A roadblock? Where the hell had that come from? Did she really believe they'd be better off apart? The mere thought of losing her left Brandt wild with possessive fury. He struggled to gather it in, to keep from exploding from the intensity of it. "No." Just that one word, pushed from between his teeth, but her reaction was instantaneous.

With an exclamation of relief, she threw her arms around his neck and kissed him with unstinting generosity. The last time she'd kissed him of her own accord—freely and openly, as herself—had been on Mazoné, and he didn't realize how desperately he missed her spontaneity, her initiating, not just responding. If he'd had their wedding night to live over, he'd never have been fooled into thinking he held Alyssa in his arms, that it was her mouth slanted beneath his. Miri put everything into her kisses and he realized she always had. She'd never been one for half measures.

He threaded his fingers into her hair, wanting a slow, thorough kiss. She gave him hot and greedy. He tried for gentle and sedate. With one teasing nip, she tumbled him into fierce and rapacious. She moaned into his mouth, the sound slamming through him, piercing straight to his heart.

When he finally lifted his head, he found her gazing up at him as though he'd just finished hanging the sun. His kiss had bee-stung her lips into plump, ripe berries, damp and parted and begging for more. He couldn't resist. He took her mouth again, only to be thrown off kilter when she gave him what he'd tried for originally. Very slow, and very thorough.

After endless minutes, she pulled back with a reluctant sigh. "Do you realize that by this time tomorrow we'll know if I'm pregnant?" Her eyes widened, filling with joyous tears. "Oh, my gosh. I might be a mother."

His arms tightened around her. "And I," he added with intense satisfaction, "will be a father."

Best of all, when her pregnancy had been confirmed, he'd be in a position to deal with the Montgomerys, once and for all. And then he'd make Miri his legally wedded bride, no matter what it took or who he had to go through in order to make it happen.

"I am sorry, Your Highness."

"So am I," Miri replied. She attempted a smile, but failed miserably. "I was so certain… Brandt and I, we both were."

The doctor touched her shoulder. "You're young. There's plenty of time to start a family. I should warn you, though. With your history of irregularity, it may take a little longer than the average couple. Just be patient. Watch your diet. Your body needs a little more weight than it's currently carrying if you want a healthy pregnancy. And try to eliminate stress from your life."

She nodded. "No more fake marriages and abductions. Got it."

The doctor's eyebrows shot skyward. "I beg your pardon?"

"Sorry. A poor attempt at a joke." She held out her hand. "Thank you for seeing me."

"With luck, you'll be back again in a few months and I'll have better news." He showed her to the door. "And my congratulations and best wishes to you and Prince Brandt. I hadn't heard that you were married."

"No, not many people have," she agreed absently. "It was a bit of surprise to everyone. Even to him."

"I see." She could tell from his confused expression that he didn't see at all, which was just as well. "Once again, Your Highness, I am sorry. I wish I had better news for you."

"So do I."

Miri left the doctor's office and crossed the parking lot to where Brandt's right-hand man, Tolken, waited with the car. Nerves skittered up and down her spine. "Thank you," she murmured as he opened the door.

She climbed into the car, fighting back tears. She'd been in a state of shock while with the doctor, but the hard, cold facts of the situation were rapidly setting in. She pressed a hand to her abdomen, feeling an emptiness there that reverberated straight to her heart. It wasn't as though she'd lost her child, she tried to reassure herself. There'd never been one to begin with. But it felt like a loss.

How would Brandt react to the news? He'd

been so pleased at the thought of a baby, so considerate and tender. What would happen once he learned she wasn't pregnant after all? Would he be disappointed, or secretly relieved? Maybe it was just as well they hadn't been sexually active since their wedding night. This way they could make decisions about their future without having to add a baby into the equation. But she couldn't help but wonder... once the truth came out, would he still want to marry her?

Or would he decide to end the relationship?

The thought leapt to her mind, unbidden. Yet the more she considered it, the more likely it seemed. It wasn't as though they were really married. Not any longer. Granted, he'd come after her that day in the parking garage, had wanted her without suspecting she might be pregnant. But what if the abduction had been out of anger? Maybe he'd wanted revenge for all she'd cost him, and it wasn't until he'd believed her pregnant that those plans had changed, that he'd considered making their marriage a real one.

She covered her face with her hands. She didn't know what to think anymore. There was only one way to find out what he intended. She'd tell him the truth. She'd tell him she wasn't pregnant and see how he reacted. And then she'd know whether she had a chance at a future with him.

"I'm sorry, Your Highness. I wish I had better news for you."

"So do I," Brandt replied with impressive calm.

"I have a full staff of accountants and lawyers ready to assist you. Say the word and we'll do everything we can to get this straightened out. How anyone could possibly believe you were working in collusion with Lauren DeVida to steal Verdonian amethysts and sell them on the black market is beyond my comprehension."

"I appreciate the support."

"Your Highness!" His man of affairs sounded shocked by the comment. "Of course we support you. We know you'd never be guilty of such an outrageous crime. It's just the timing. The timing is quite unfortunate."

Now there was an understatement if he'd ever heard one. Brandt suppressed a laugh, not that it would have held any amusement. "The timing isn't unfortunate. It's impeccable." Too impeccable. "If you're a Montgomery."

There was a moment of appalled silence. Then, "I see. I'll get someone on this right away."

"Thank you, Maitrim."

Brandt hung up the phone with a grimace. He suspected that any number of "someones" could be put on the problem and it still wouldn't be resolved. Not until after the election. And maybe not even then.

He poured himself a drink while he considered his options. But instead of sipping the single malt, he stared into the amber liquid as though it held the answers to his questions. If it weren't for Miri's pregnancy, his decision would be a simple one. Honor. Duty. Responsibility. Sacrifice. It was his duty to protect the baby he'd created, equally his duty to protect Miri. Unfortunately, the two had just become mutually exclusive.

In order to protect his child, he had to marry the mother. In order to protect Miri, he had to send her away. So, who held the greatest claim to duty and responsibility? He swirled the whiskey in his glass. He knew what his grandfather would say. The baby was his top priority because it was the most helpless and innocent. If it weren't for the child… He downed his drink in a single swallow. Thank God for the pregnancy, because it narrowed his choices to one. If it weren't for the baby, he'd be honor-bound to protect Miri from the coming storm.

It would be his duty to sacrifice what he desired most.

CHAPTER EIGHT

As soon as Brandt set eyes on Miri he realized that something had gone terribly wrong. Had she found out about the charges being leveled against him? Or was it even worse than that? He shot to his feet. The baby! Please, God, don't let anything be wrong with their baby. After all that had transpired in the past twenty-four hours, their child had been the one good thing he could hold on to.

"What is it, sweetheart?" He circled the desk and wrapped his arms around her. "Is it the pregnancy? Has something happened to the baby?" he questioned urgently.

She shook her head, her eyes huge and dark and filling with tears. "I'm sorry, Brandt."

Her chin quivered and a tear fell, sliding down her pale cheek. "I was wrong. I'm not pregnant."

"Shh." He tucked her close and held her while she cried it out. "I'm sorry. I know how inadequate that sounds. But I am so sorry. I'd hoped—"

And so had she. Clearly, she'd wanted the baby as much as he had and he couldn't help but celebrate that fact, even as he mourned the loss of the child he'd spent the past two days imagining. He'd wanted to have a baby with Miri, had looked forward to its advent in his life. And now he realized that not only was that an impossibility, it would never happen in the future. He'd make sure of that. In one brief second he'd gone from having it all, to losing everything.

Brandt steeled himself for what would have to come next. Now that he knew for a fact that Miri wasn't pregnant, his choices had changed. He had a responsibility toward her. Honor and duty required him to protect her. And to protect her meant sending her home. There was no way he could do that without hurting her. But maybe it was just as well. If he hurt her, she'd be willing to leave. She'd *want* to leave.

He cleared his throat. "This seems to be the day for news, both good and bad."

She lifted her head from his shoulder. "Which is the baby?" she whispered, her undisguised pain threatening to rip his heart from his chest. "Good or bad?"

"Do you have to ask?" He smoothed the hair from her face and knuckled a tear from cheek. "I'm sorry there's no baby. I'd already made our child a part of my life. A part of our future."

Her breath caught in a sob. "So had I."

"There's something I need to tell you, Miri."

"The good?"

"Yes, the good." It cost him to keep his expression encouraging, to act pleased with his news. "Now that our marriage has been annulled and there's no baby, you're free to return home."

Her brows drew together. "How is that good news?"

Excellent question. "It's good because I won't be holding you here against your will any longer. I'm sure your family will be relieved about that. They feel, as do I, that it's inappropriate for you to remain here, given the circumstances."

She stared at him in disbelief. "You said Avernos was my home. You said we would remarry if the annulment went through."

"That's when we thought you were pregnant."

"The baby?" She tore free of his arms and took a stumbling step backward. "The baby was the only reason for us to marry? Is that what you're telling me?"

He hardened himself against the disbelief in her face. "I brought you here against your will, as you've told me on more than one occasion. Now I'm letting you go. It's the right thing."

"Please, Brandt. Don't do this. I don't know what's going on, but I…" Defiance radiated from her. "I won't go. Not until you tell me the real reason you're sending me away. Is it my family? Are they threatening you?"

He had one final card to play, one he'd hoped to avoid using. His hands balled into fists. One guaranteed to work. "I repeat. I brought you here believing we were still married. It's inappropriate for you to be here now that we're not. It's not just your reputation at stake. There's still the election to consider."

It only took a minute for that to sink in. The instant it did, the breath exploded from her lungs. "This is about winning the election? You're sending me away because…because what? Having me in your bed when we're not married might cost you some votes? You want to be king so badly that you'd sacrifice our life together to get it?"

He shoved out his response between gritted teeth. "Yes."

She stood there for an endless moment, as though waiting for him to take it back. Bit by bit her hope died a slow death, while he died inch by inch watching it. Finally her chin shot up. "Fine. If that's what's most important, you can choke on your damned crown. I'll go pack."

He retreated behind a regal facade. "Thank you. I'll arrange for your flight home. Tolken will inform you when the helicopter is ready to depart."

Miri turned on her heel and walked from the room, her head held high, despite feeling as though her life had just ended. It wasn't until she'd reached the hallway that she lost control. Helpless tears streamed down her cheeks. She ignored them, forcing her feet to keep moving, step after step, until she'd gained the privacy of their bedroom.

For endless minutes she stood in the middle of the room, looking around in bewilderment. She'd told Brandt she'd go and pack but she didn't have anything *to* pack. None of the clothes littering the closet belonged to her, though she'd bet her last dollar that Brandt wouldn't agree. Gifts, he'd call them. Well, she refused to take anything he'd purchased for her. She'd leave as she arrived.

The thought gave her direction, sending her flying to the closet. It didn't take long to find the clothes she'd worn when she, Juliana and Alyssa had donned disguises and snuck out of the palace for their shopping trip to the mall. Was it only two short days earlier? It seemed decades ago.

After washing her face, she changed into the slacks and tee she'd been wearing that day, and braided her hair in preparation for the trip home. She was just gathering up her purse when her cell phone rang. She checked the incoming number and almost burst into tears again when she saw her mother's name displayed.

"Mom?"

"I've just heard," Rachel said without pre-amble. "Are you all right?"

Miri sank onto the edge of the mattress. "I don't understand. How did you find out so fast? Who told you? Did Brandt call?"

"No, no. It was Lander. He got it from the Temporary Governing Council. Oh, honey. He's very worried. He's offering to help in any way he can."

What? Miri lifted a hand to her throbbing temple. That didn't make sense. How could the TGC know about her pregnancy? "I don't understand. What's Lander got to do with—" Something didn't add up. "Let's start over. Why are you calling?"

"I heard about the allegations against Brandt, of course."

"What allegations?"

"Don't you know?" Rachel made an impa-tient sound. "Unbelievable. He probably thinks he's protecting you. That's his grandfather's influence, no doubt. Typical Verdonian man."

Miri's grip tightened on the phone. "Mom, for heaven's sake! What are you talking about?"

"I'm talking about the charges that are being leveled against Prince Brandt," came the crisp response. "They're claiming he was working in collusion with Lauren DeVida to steal the amethysts and sell them on the black market. Ridiculous, of course."

Miri shot to her feet. "That's outrageous. Who's claiming Brandt's involved? Who's made these allegations?"

"The Temporary Governing Council. New evidence has come to their attention."

"What evidence? Where? From whom?"

"I don't know. Lander's trying to find out."

"Well, I'm telling you it's impossible." Realizing she was shouting into the phone, Miri attempted to modulate her voice. "Brandt would never steal from anyone, certainly not the country he's sworn to protect. Not ever. Honor and duty are as much a part of him as blood and bone."

There was a long pause, and then Rachel said, "You love him, don't you?"

The gentleness in her mother's voice almost proved Miri's undoing. "Yes. I love him." It took her a moment before she could continue, to gather her self-control sufficiently to think straight. "He's sending me away, Mom. Our marriage has been annulled and since I'm not pregnant—"

"Pregnant!"

"Are you listening to me? I said *not* pregnant."

"Yes, I hear you." Rachel sighed. "As I said before, honey, it's clear that he's trying to protect you by sending you away. Obviously, he doesn't want your reputation tarnished by all this nastiness."

Was it possible? Miri sank back onto the edge of the bed. It was more than possible. Probable, bordering on definite. "Well, I'm not leaving him. Not now."

"He's not an easy man to thwart," Rachel

pointed out. "And he can be very persuasive when he chooses."

Something in her mother's tone caught Miri's attention. "Just out of curiosity, how would you know all that?"

There was an awkward pause before Rachel replied. "Oh, all right. If you must know, Brandt convinced me to tell him when you would be away from the palace so he could contact you. He said he wanted to try and resolve your differences," she admitted reluctantly. "A fat lot of good that did. First he abducts you, and now he's sending you back again as if you were an article of clothing that didn't fit right. The nerve of that man!"

Miri keyed in on the most vital part of her mother's diatribe. "*You* told him where to find me?" She could scarcely believe it.

Rachel cleared her throat. "You were so upset," she attempted to explain. "In so much pain. Even if things didn't work out between you, at least you'd have made the effort. Darn it, Miri. I meant well."

"I know you did, Mom. To be honest, I'm sitting here debating whether or not to thank you."

"You say thank you, and I'll say you're welcome, and we'll consider the subject closed. Now, how are you planning to fix this mess?"

Good question. "Give me a minute. I'm thinking." Miri rubbed her forehead. "The first thing I need is for Juliana to take a look at whatever evidence the TGC has and see if she can figure out what's going on. She found the discrepancy with Lander and cleared his name, maybe she can do the same for Brandt. Do you think she'd be willing to help?"

"She'll help. I guarantee it."

"Perfect. In the meantime, I intend to take a page out of Merrick's book."

"Oh, Lord. I'm almost afraid to ask."

"I'm going to abduct my ex-husband." Miri

smiled grimly. "All things considered, it only seems fair, don't you think?"

Brandt tossed down his pen. "What do you mean she won't leave?"

Tolken shrugged. "Her Highness says she won't leave unless you accompany her."

"We'll see about that." Brandt thrust the papers he'd been working on into a folder and stood. Snagging his suit jacket from the back of his chair, he shrugged into it. "Let's go."

He found his wife—no, not his wife, he reminded himself—waiting on the lawn near the helo pad. She stood quietly off to one side, wearing a simple pair of bronze-colored slacks and a matching tee. She'd swept her hair back from her face and restrained it in a simple braid down her back. For some reason seeing her standing there, so small against the backdrop of the helicopter, with a single suitcase at her feet, made her appear delicate and helpless and lost. It took everything he possessed not to gather

her up and return her to their bedroom and to say to hell with honor and duty and responsibility.

He fought to remind himself that Miri was anything but delicate, helpless, or lost. But that didn't curb his urge to head for the bedroom with her. He crossed to her side. "What's going on?" he questioned briskly. "What's wrong?"

"Nothing's wrong. I just informed Tolken I wouldn't leave unless you escorted me." She lifted an eyebrow in a regal manner. "All things considered, I think it's the least you can do. Don't you?"

He briefly considered arguing the point. But if agreeing to accompany her meant her prompt return to Verdon, without further debate or discussion, he'd go along with it. "Fine. I'll escort you home." He snagged her suitcase and gestured toward the helicopter. "Shall we?"

He'd half expected her to refuse to take any of the clothes he'd purchased for her, and it relieved his mind to see her being reasonable about it. Even though barely a quarter of the clothes filling her closet could have fit in her suitcase, at least a few of the items wouldn't go to waste. Tolken had them both on board in short order and as soon as he'd made certain everyone was strapped in, he joined the pilot and they went airborne.

Miri sat decorously at his side, hands folded in her lap, gaze focused straight ahead, and Brandt eyed her with deep suspicion. This was too easy. She had to be up to something. Before he had time to consider the endless possibilities for someone so impulsive, Tolken spoke to him through the headphones.

"There's a problem, Your Highness. The pilot believes something's wrong with the fuel line. He's looking for a place to set down while he checks it out."

"There's a clearing not far from here." Brandt shot Miri a concerned glance. His plan had been to get her out of harm's way, not put her in it. "Have him watch for a lake slightly north of our position. There's a cabin and boathouse at one end. There should be room to land there."

The helicopter gave a slight stutter, than banked sharply in the direction he'd indicated. Within minutes the lake came into view. With smooth precision, the pilot landed not far from the cabin, recommending as he did so that they exit the craft and stretch their legs while he ran through his inspection. Brandt unfastened his seat belt, and Miri and Tolken followed suit.

"How long will it take to diagnose the problem?" Brandt asked, once they'd moved clear of the churning blades.

Tolken frowned. "I'm not certain, Your Highness. I'll check with the pilot and give you a full report as soon as possible. If it's going to take too long, I'll call for a car. Would it be possible to borrow your cell phone? Mine doesn't seem to be working."

Brandt nodded, handing it over. "Yes, of course." He was so relieved that Miri was safe, he didn't care how long it took them to fix the blasted thing. If need be, he'd drive her all the way to Verdon.

"I'll return as soon as possible," Tolken said and trotted back to the helicopter.

Miri touched Brandt's arm and gestured toward the cabin. "This seems familiar. Have I been here before?"

Turning his back on the helicopter, he gave her an odd look. "Don't you remember?"

She shook her head. "No, actually I don't." She started across the knee-high grass in the direction of the cabin and he fell in step beside her. "When was I here? It must have been ages ago."

"Fifteen years, maybe a few more. I'm surprised you don't recall. This is where I rescued—"

Before he could finish, a loud escalating whine sounded behind them. Spinning around he watched in disbelief as the helicopter rose skyward. It hovered for a brief moment directly overhead, then banked to the south and vanished behind the tree line. All that remained in its place was Miri's suitcase. It sat in the middle of a circle of flattened grass, an incongruous monument to his massive stupidity.

Cold anger bit deep and he turned it on Miri. "What the hell is going on?"

"We needed to talk in private, where you couldn't either walk out on me or send me away." She shrugged. "Tolken was kind enough to assist."

"Tolken is fired."

To his fury, she didn't appear the least concerned. "Merrick will be happy to pick him up. He's been trying to lure Tolken away from you for years."

"This is ridiculous." He searched his pockets for his cell phone, swearing beneath his breath when he remembered what he'd done with it. "There's nothing left to be said between us. You're returning home now that there's no reason for us to remain together, and that's the end of it."

She planted her hands on her hips. "Honor. Duty. Responsibility. How does sending me away jive with those?" Her eyes narrowed. "Or does it jive with another of those lessons you learned at your grandfather's knee? Maybe this has to do with sacrifice."

"This has to do with the fact that you're not pregnant and we're not married and—" Damn it to hell! What was the other thing? She had him so worked up he couldn't think straight anymore. Oh, right. "And it has to do with my plans to steal the bloody throne from your bloody brother!"

She actually had the nerve to approach and poke a finger into his chest. "I don't believe you. All that talk about the baby and a future together was just that? Talk?"

His mouth compressed. "I'm sorry. I know we discussed a future. But this is a better option."

She shook her head in disgust. "It's clear I have my work cut out for me." Tramping across the grass, she snagged her suitcase and then headed for the cabin.

"I don't have a key," he called after her.

"I do."

He bit off a word that would have gotten his face slapped if Miri had heard. He could practically feel the frustration leaking out of his ears as she continued on her merry way, impervious to his wrath. Unlocking the cabin, she had to shove at the door to get it open and he made a mental note to have it sanded at the first opportunity.

After a minute's hesitation, he followed. "I'm going to ask you again, Miri. What are you doing?"

She moved through the main room of the cabin, throwing open windows to air the place out. A light breeze poured in through the screens, causing the lightweight curtains to flutter like flags of surrender. "What I'm doing is waiting for an explanation."

What was it about her? No other woman, hell,

no other person he came into contact with on a daily basis, had the nerve to confront and push and demand the way Miri did. Didn't she understand? He spoke; she obeyed. That's how it worked. That's how it had always worked. It was that simple. He'd told her to leave, told her in the most brutal fashion possible. Why was she still here, torturing him? He needed her safe so he could deal with the charges against him, so he could focus on what was to come.

"This is pointless, Miri," he informed her harshly. "There is nothing left for us to say to each other."

"Really?" She paused in her examination of the cabin and confronted him, folding her arms across her chest. "What about the allegations against you? Theft of the amethysts, or some such? That should give us plenty to talk about."

He clamped his teeth together, literally seeing red. "How did you find out?" he ground out.

"Your spy is a turncoat. But then, that's what happens when you use my mother. She's susceptible to being flipped." Miri swept a hand in the air. "Past loyalties and all that."

He forked his fingers through his hair, fighting a losing battle to recover his self-control. "What do you want from me?"

She hesitated in front of him, her impudence fading, replaced by a sincerity that just about killed him. "I'd like the opportunity to stand by you, if you'll let me."

He had no idea how he managed to shake his head, let alone speak past the emotions clogging his throat. But he did it. "That's not going to happen."

"We'll see." She marched into the kitchen and started poking and prodding through the cupboards. "I have three days to change your mind."

If he could have gotten his hands on Tolken in that minute, he'd have done serious damage. "Three days? I don't have three days, I have charges pending against me in case you've forgotten."

"There's nothing more you can do that isn't already being done on your behalf by people determined to prove your innocence. If anything critical happens, Tolken will come and get us." She moved from the cupboards to the pantry, checking the status of their supplies. "He said the cabin is well stocked, as is the lake. We won't starve, that's for sure." She smiled, as though she didn't have a care in the world. "I'm hungry. Why don't I see what there is to eat. I don't suppose there's a freezer around here?"

Brandt shook his head. "No electricity."

She actually brightened at that. "Are you serious? How romantic."

Romantic? Oh, no. Not romantic. Not if he could help it. He'd make sure of that, no matter what it took. Rage continued to burn within, desperate for an outlet, but he fought to restrain it. There'd be ample time to confront Miri over forcing him into this situation. But not now. Not with fury hovering on the bare edge of control. Stripping off his suit coat, he flung it over the nearest chair before rolling up his shirt sleeves. "If we're going to stay here tonight, we're going to need kerosene lamps. And flashlights. I'll take care of that, if you'll throw something together to eat. I'll also set up the bedrooms."

He started down the hallway, but her question stopped him in his tracks. "Just to clarify. Did you say bedrooms, plural?"

Oh, yeah. "Very plural."

"Okay, but fair warning. Plural is pointless, unless you're planning to lock your bedroom door."

"I'll nail it shut if that's what it takes." He kept his back to her. It seemed safer that way. "You're not pregnant, Miri. When we leave here you'll still not be pregnant."

"If that's the way you want it."

It wasn't. "It is."

"Okay. You take care of the bedrooms,

plural. I'll see what I can put together for dinner. Then we can finish fighting."

She was as good as her word. The moment their dinner dishes were cleared away, she started in on him again. "All this quiet and solitude will give us plenty of opportunity to straighten out our differences." A gentle lob for a first sally.

"Differences?" Was the woman insane? "We don't have any differences. What we have here is a blatant disregard for the obvious." Darkness was fast descending and he lined up a trio of kerosene lamps. After trimming the wicks, he lit them, adjusting the brightness to a non-romantic level. "Let me make this simple. We can stay here three hours, three days, or three years, and it's not going to change anything. You're going home where you'll be out of the line of fire."

She picked up one of the lamps and carried it to a small end table centered between the two windows in the main section of the cabin. "I thought I was going home because you wanted the bloody throne. Or are you finally willing to admit the real reason?"

"Feel free to pick any reason you want, if it means you'll return to Verdon."

She crossed the room to stand in front of him. The nonromantic lamp light gave her skin a pearly sheen and lost itself in the soft green of her eyes. It even made her mouth seem fuller, rosier, and her hair richer, darker. "Please, Brandt." She rested a hand on his arm. "All I want is the truth."

Maybe if she hadn't touched him, he'd have been able to resist. But that one simple caress had him giving her what she wanted. "Fine. The truth is that I won't let you stay in Avernos, Miri. I won't let you run the risk of being tarnished by the accusations against me. Nor will I have a child of ours born under a cloud of suspicion."

She frowned. "I don't understand. You were willing to marry me if I'd been pregnant."

He conceded the point with a nod. "Our baby needed the protection of my name, more than you needed the protection of distance from me. Now that a baby is no longer an issue, you've become my top priority. I won't allow suspicion to fall on you. And I won't have you married to a man who could spend the rest of his days in prison. You'd have the responsibility for all of Avernos. You'd have to give up your life to take over my duties. I won't tie you to that. It's too much."

"That's my choice."

"You're wrong. It's mine."

A hint of irritation gleamed in her eyes. "Lander tried this very same thing with Juliana. He didn't want her touched by the scandal that erupted when you took your accusations against him before the TGC. He tried to keep her in Texas while he faced the charges. He wouldn't let anyone tell her what had happened."

Brandt winced. "I didn't know."

"She didn't tolerate it and neither will I."

"It's not your choice. Lander and Juliana were married." He braced himself to hurt her. "We're not."

Her mouth formed a stubborn line. "Fine. Be that way. Not that it matters. None of this will be a problem much longer."

"You can't know that."

"Actually, I can," she retorted. "I have Juliana looking into the accusations as we speak. By the time Tolken returns I expect to have all this resolved."

He froze. "What did you say?"

She must have picked up on something in his reaction because her eyes widened and for the first time that day she seemed wary of his temper. "I said Juliana is looking into the charges. Like she did with Lander."

"You brought your family into this?" he asked in a soft voice.

"You're…you're my husband. Legally or not."

She fell back a pace, as though scenting danger. "Of course, I brought my family into it."

He stalked closer. "First, I'm not your husband. Chances are excellent I never will be. Second, you had no business involving the Montgomerys in this. Considering their culpability in the financial crisis Verdonia is facing, I don't want them anywhere near me or my problems. Is that clear?"

Color ebbed from her face. "Crystal. One question."

"Ask."

"When you say 'Montgomery' like that, as though you despise the very name, does that include me?"

"Of course not. I don't—"

"Good. Because in case you've forgotten, I'm a Montgomery, too. Or perhaps I don't count because I'm not one by birth." She lifted her chin. "Is that why you tolerate me? Because I'm not a real Montgomery?"

"I don't tolerate you. I mean—"

"*That* has become painfully obvious." Snatching up one of the kerosene lamps, she stalked to her bedroom and slammed the door behind her.

Damn it! That wasn't what he meant and she knew it. This was her infuriating way of putting an end to an argument when she was clearly in the wrong. Involving her family. Claiming she wasn't a real Montgomery. Come morning he'd have a thing or two to say on those subjects. And with another couple days of blissful togetherness, he'd make sure she heard, loud and clear, even if he had to blissful her backside. Grabbing up the mate to her kerosene lamp, Brandt headed for his own bedroom, reasonably confident that he wouldn't need locks or nails to keep her out of his bed. And if his door shut just shy of a slam, she could blame it on the wind.

Out in the main room of the cabin, the wind did blow. The lightweight curtains caught each gust, swirling in their own private dance. They danced well into the night, danced like moths drawn to the bright flame that came from the kerosene lamp that sat on the table between them.

They danced until their wings were singed and they finally caught fire.

CHAPTER NINE

MIRI never knew what woke her. Perhaps it was the sound, a continuous and intense snap and pop that disturbed her sleep because it was so out of place. Perhaps it was the odor, the insidious permeation of smoke where no smoke should exist. Or perhaps intuition had her bolting upright in bed, going from unconsciousness to wide-eyed wakefulness in the span of a few disorienting seconds. Whatever the reason, the instant she came to, it was with the gut-level certainty that something had gone seriously wrong.

Scurrying from the bed, she ran to the door, remembering just in time to check the knob for heat before opening it. The metal blistered her fingertips and she jerked her hand back, retreating across the room. For endless seconds she stood there, the sound of her breath jackhammering in and out of her lungs so loud she couldn't think straight.

Stay calm! she ordered herself. She couldn't afford to panic. She needed to get a grip and figure out the best way to deal with the emergency. "Brandt," she whispered.

Why wasn't he here? He had to still be asleep or he'd have beaten down the door to get to her. Oh, God! Could his inaction be due to something more serious? Could the smoke have already reached his room? Was he unconscious? Suffocating, while she stood here in a daze? She had to move. Now.

Spinning around, she darted to the window. Endless seconds were wasted as she struggled to unlock it and then pry it open. Age, humidity and a recent paint job made it a struggle, which was why she hadn't opened it earlier. The crackle from the outer room of the cabin grew louder, nearly a roar, and she threw a swift, fearful glance over her shoulder.

To her horror, wisps of smoke slipped beneath the door. She finally managed to raise the window as far as it would go, but a screen blocked her egress and she shoved at it with all her strength. It bowed outward, then popped free of the frame. With more speed than grace, she tumbled through the opening onto the porch that surrounded the cabin. Leaping to her feet, she ran to the window adjacent to her own, pounding frantically on it. The screen deadened the noise.

"Brandt!" she shouted. "Brandt, the cabin's on fire. Wake up!"

No response. There could only be one reason. He'd passed out from smoke inhalation. Fleeing the porch, she searched in the dark for a rock or stick large enough to break the window. She managed to find a decent-sized stone by stubbing her toe on it. Limping back to the porch, she heaved the rock at the window with all her might. It ripped through the screen and shattered the glass beyond.

Smoke poured from the opening, and with a sudden, ferocious explosion of heat and light, flames flashed through the room with a deafening howl, consuming everything in their path. The intensity of it drove Miri back. Sobbing, screaming herself hoarse, she circled the burning cabin, hoping against hope that Brandt would come stumbling from the building in the nick of time. But with each passing minute, hope faded, and likelihood became impossibility.

Flames shot skyward, erupting from every window now and eating through the roof. There wasn't a part of the cabin that wasn't fully on fire, no safe place for a person to escape from. Tripping over the dragging hem of her nightgown, Miri fell heavily to the ground.

No. No, Brandt couldn't be dead. She couldn't go on if she lost him. She loved him, loved him more than she thought it possible to love another human being. He couldn't be gone. Life wouldn't do that to them. Not now. Not when they'd come here to work out their differences. She began to shake. Not when *she'd* forced them to come here.

But staring at the raging inferno, she knew that no one could still be inside that and survive. Hopelessness consumed her. Brandt was dead, probably gone from smoke inhalation before she'd even awoken. She was a fool to pretend otherwise. This was her fault, all her fault for thinking she could force him to love her. That she could force him to acknowledge feelings that weren't there and never would be. Dragging herself away from the heat and rain of hot ash, she huddled beneath a nearby tree, curling into a tight ball of utter desolation.

And then she wept, deep, helpless sobs that came from the very heart and soul of her.

Brandt pointed the beam of the flashlight along the path in front of him, hoping a lap around the lake would exhaust him enough that he could sleep instead of picturing Miri alone in her bed without him. He was a fool. A fool to have abducted her. A fool to have kept her. And even more of a fool for sending her away again.

He glanced toward the lake to check his position. Almost exactly halfway around and nowhere near exhausted enough for sleep. Maybe he'd need a second lap around. Or a third. He caught a flash out of the corner of his eyes, a flicker of light that didn't belong, and paused for a closer look. Clicking off his flashlight, he peered through the darkness.

It only took a minute to comprehend what he was seeing. On the far side of the lake a deep orange glow erupted through the trees. There was only one thing that could cause that. A fire.

"Miri." He swore violently. "Please, God, no. Not Miri."

Flicking on the flashlight, he ran, flat out.

Brambles and branches overgrowing the path reached out to snare him, ripping at his clothes and tripping him. He didn't slow. Roots. Rocks. Logs. He flew over every obstacle, keeping his eyes focused on the path ahead as he pounded the endless distance back. Every step of the way he could see the flames from the periphery of his vision, and could tell the fire was building in intensity. And he knew, no matter how hard he tried to deny it, that he wouldn't make it back in time. He'd be too late to save her.

She was dying as he ran. And it was all his fault. If he'd stayed. If they hadn't fought. If he'd been willing to take her to his bed and give her one last night of love, she'd be alive. But he hadn't done any of those things. Hell, no. He'd been determined to face the accusations on his own, to protect her from the public outcry. God, what irony. Instead of protecting her, he'd killed her.

He dashed sweat from his eyes and raced on. Maybe she woke in time. Maybe she got out.

Maybe she escaped unscathed. She had to be alive. She had to. He couldn't survive without her. The litany ran in a desperate loop, ran in pace with the driving thud of his footfalls. And all the while the cabin burned, a ferocious testament to his failure.

He could barely pull air into his lungs by the time he reached the clearing where the cabin stood—or rather, the conflagration that had once been a cabin. He desperately scanned the area, searching for some sign of life, some sign of Miri. There was nothing. He shouted her name but got no answer. No one burst joyously from the darkness. No one raced to throw herself into his arms. There was only the roar of a hungry fire.

Brandt needed to get away from here, clear his head and lungs of smoke. But he couldn't leave. Not yet. Not without Miri. He straightened and began another circuit, slower this time. Heavier.

Up ahead something white flickered beneath

the trees and he stared at it dully. An animal crouched near the flames. No, that didn't make sense. Animals ran from fire. Only humans were foolish enough to embrace it.

The crumpled heap of white stirred. "Brandt?" His name escaped in a disbelieving quaver. "Is it really you?"

Joy burned hotter than the fire, shooting through him like quicksilver. "Miri? Oh, God. Miri!" He raced across the singed grass. Scooping her up in his arms, he sagged to his knees, his hands sweeping over her face and shoulders, her torso and legs. "Are you hurt? Are you burned? Talk to me, sweetheart. Are you okay?"

"No, yes. I'm fine. I'm fine." She cupped his face with shaking hands, her words barely coherent. "Where were you? I called and called and you never answered. I thought you were—" Her voice broke and she wept helplessly, tears tracking sooty lines down her face. "I thought I'd lost you."

"I went for a walk. I was clear across the lake when I saw the flames." He rained kisses down on her face. "You have no idea how I felt when I saw the fire. When I realized I'd never get to you in time."

"Don't leave me. Don't let go."

"Never. Never again."

He wrapped her up in his arms, holding her so close he could feel her heart pounding in rhythm with his own. Beyond them the cabin continued to burn, the snap and pop of the wood mingled with an occasional ping of exploding nails. Heat radiated from the blaze. And yet, they remained crouched in the grass, clinging to each other. It wasn't until the wind shifted, blowing soot and ash in their direction that he felt compelled to move.

Helping Miri to her feet, Brandt urged her in the direction of the lake. "Come on. Let's get cleaned up."

"We don't have anything to change into." She

glanced over her shoulder, shuddering. "All our clothes are burned."

"There are towels in the boathouse. We can rinse the soot out of what we're wearing and wrap up in towels while our clothes dry."

He heard her take a deep breath and could literally see her gathering up her self-control. It showed in the stiffening of her spine and her proud carriage, the squaring of her jaw and the way she planted her hands on her hips. He could only shake his head as he watched, amazed at the undaunted perseverance that was such a natural part of her.

She scanned the area. "Is there a stream that feeds the lake?"

"A quarter of the way around," he confirmed.

She nodded. "We can get fresh water from there. And I'll bet if you have towels stashed in the boathouse, there'll be fishing poles, too. We may have to rough it until help arrives, but we won't starve or die of thirst."

He smiled at the proof that her spirit had returned. It was one of the qualities he'd always admired about her. Nothing kept Miri down for long. They picked their way across the wild grass to the boathouse, only to discover a large padlock barring their entry.

"Forgot about this," he said. "Hang on."

He circled the structure until he found a decent-sized stone he could use to hammer off the lock. It only took a half dozen whacks before the clasp broke. Tossing the pieces aside, he opened the door. It was pitch-black inside.

"I don't suppose there's a light switch?" she asked.

"No. And I seem to have lost the flashlight I had earlier. But I vaguely remember keeping extras on a shelf just inside the door. Ah, here they are. Now if the batteries are still good." The first was dead. The second emitted a weak beam that lasted long enough for them to collect a stack of towels and a tarp. "Come on.

Let's get rinsed off. Then we'll set up a bed for the night."

He led the way to a narrow beach adjacent to the boathouse, a sweeping sickle of imported white sand far softer than the rock-strewn ground closer to the cabin. He spread the tarp and padded it with towels.

Miri had wandered to the lake's edge where the water lapped her bare feet. Overhead the moon sent a halo of silver spilling over her. A light wind stirred, wafting her soot-stained nightgown against her legs, outlining their shapely length, and lifting her hair in a rippling ebony flag. A flag of triumph, of survival. She glanced over her shoulder and tossed him a teasing grin. Then facing the lake, she waded in, looking like some sort of mythical sea nymph returning to her watery home.

She gave a small gasp as she sank to her waist, no doubt reacting to the chilly temperature. Then with a light splash that echoed across the lake, she vanished beneath the surface. He didn't wait any longer to join her. Toeing off his shoes, he crossed the sand at a dead run and dove toward where he'd seen her go under.

They surfaced side by side, almost on top of each other. "Refreshing," he said, pulling her into his arms.

Her nightgown swirled around them, then clung, anchoring them together. "More like freezing." She scooped water into her hands and washed the grime from his face and neck, scrubbing at a spot just beneath his jaw. Her fingers slowed. Lingered. Traced the harsh planes and angles of his face as though they were the most beautiful sight in the world. "There. Much better."

He pointed to the corner of his mouth. "You missed a spot."

"So I did." Using his shoulders for leverage, she surged upward long enough to kiss the place he'd indicated. "I think I got it."

Not even close. But she would soon enough. "Your turn," he informed her.

Settling his feet on the lake bottom, he started with her face, skimming deftly across her forehead, then down her nose and finally across her arching cheekbones. He paused at her lips, replaced his hands with his mouth, and kissed her. Inhaled her. Lost himself in the honeyed flavor of her.

"I don't know what I'd have done if I'd lost you," he said, the words rough with emotion.

She buried her face against the crook of his shoulder. "Watching the cabin burn, believing you were trapped inside…" He could hear the traces of horror lingering in her voice. "I've never been more frightened in my life."

He gathered the wet nightgown tangled around her and in one smooth motion, pulled it over her head and tossed it to the lakeshore. Now that they'd rinsed their clothes, they didn't need them anymore. He let go of her just long enough to strip off his slacks and shirt before sending them chasing after her nightgown.

"Shouldn't we hang those—" she began.

"No, we shouldn't. There are more important things for us to do tonight than hang laundry."

Catching her hand in his, he drew her back into his embrace. Their bodies collided, wet and slippery. Everything about her was soft. Her mouth, full and moist and hungry. Her breasts, the water breaking across the generous slopes. Her abdomen. He grazed that feminine curve, remembering what it had felt like when he'd believed his child lay there, tucked safely within her womb.

Her legs scissored at the unexpected contact, sending her bobbing upward. "I can't touch the bottom."

"You don't need to." He hooked his hands behind the backs of her upper thighs and parted her legs, sliding between them. "Hold on to me, love."

She shuddered in his grasp, her muscles spasming at the tantalizing brush of flesh against flesh. Masculine against feminine. "Please," she moaned, her eyes fluttering closed. "Say my name, Brandt. Make love to *me* this time."

"Look at me, Miri." He fisted his hands in her hair, waiting until she complied. "That's right, sweetheart. Look at me, just like I'm looking at you. I know who I'm holding. And whether you believe it or not, some part of me knew who it was on our wedding night."

Her chin wobbled. "It wasn't our wedding night. It was yours and Alyssa's."

"You're wrong." How could he make her understand? "I thought I could forget about you. That I could marry Alyssa and put you out of my life. But it wouldn't have worked. The minute I would have tried to make love to her—the real Alyssa—it would have turned to ashes." He spun her around to face the fire. "Look at it. You and I, we're that blaze. That's what happens when we touch. Alyssa and I would have been the cold ash we'll find over there come morning."

"You called me by her name." She treaded

water, allowing a chilly gap to form between them. Moonbeams caught in her eyes and highlighted her pain. "That was the last word you spoke to me."

"I'm sorry. It was never my intention to hurt you."

"You did."

So simple. So direct. He'd broken something he wasn't sure he could repair. "Listen to me, sweetheart. It wasn't Alyssa in that bed with me on our wedding night, anymore than it was Alyssa standing beside me at the altar when we spoke our vows."

"The church has annulled our marriage," she interrupted. "Those vows are meaningless."

"They're not meaningless. Not to us." The words, loud and vehement, echoed across the lake, silencing the nighttime chatter coming from the surrounding woods. He caught hold of her hand and towed her closer. "The church may not recognize our union, but I recognize it. And so do you."

Slowly, the evening songs resumed. High-pitched insect strumming and trilling birdcall, the bass accompaniment of nearby amphibians, as well as the light clatter of branches, called to life by an insistent breeze. He kissed her to the sound of that music, a kiss as tender and sacred as if they were standing once again in front of an altar.

"Admit it, Miri. In your heart, you're married to me. That's why you refuse to give up on us. That's why you have Juliana working to clear my name. We're joined, in every way it's possible for a man and woman to be joined."

He sealed the words with another kiss, this one more ardent. He could feel the longing in her, taste her yearning. What he wanted, though, was her passion. And then it came, bursting from her, hot and demanding and unconditional. That one kiss nearly devastated his self-control. He fought to hold on, determined to make this the most special night of her life. He owed her that much at least.

He drifted toward shore with her, his caresses following the shallowing waterline. He kissed the moisture from the taut sweep of her neck, then the slope of her shoulders. He followed the length of her arms, all the way to her fingertips, before cupping her breasts and lavishing teeth and tongue on each pebbled tip. He skated lower still as they reached the shore, catching the beads of moisture that slid down her belly.

Sinking to his knees, he held her upright while he traced a line from the womanly flare of her right hip across her soft belly to her left. He could just make out the jeweled butterfly that fluttered there. It took on a whole new meaning—a testament to their time on Mazoné. Where before he'd avoided it, this time he gave it his full attention. Satisfied, he steadied her before sinking lower, finding the very heart of her.

Her entire body reverberated, burning like an inferno as intense as the fire still roaring behind them. She arched backward until her hair swirled in the water, the strands wrapping around them, binding them together. She went bowstring taut, her throat working in a silent shriek. He pushed her higher. Harder. With a breathless cry, she tipped over the edge, the breath gusting from her lungs. And then she folded, collapsing in his arms, trembling in re-action.

Turning, he beached them and gathered her close. The storm raging through her abated, but only for the moment. Not giving her time to do more than catch her breath, he drove her upward again.

"I know who I'm holding in my arms. It's you, Miri. Only you."

Possessiveness burned in her gaze, filling him with an urgent desire to touch every part of her, to take his time feasting on every inch. He reared upward, baring her to his gaze. The moonlight tracked across her damp body, a glistening swathe of silver. She lay open to him, her eyes dark with want. The air shuddered from her lungs, preventing speech. Instead, she reached for him, impatience implicit in every movement as she tugged him into her waiting embrace.

"Easy, love," he murmured.

"I don't want easy." She sealed his mouth with a hard, greedy kiss. "I want out of control. I want you to show me that I'm the only woman who can make you feel like this."

"Don't you know?" He smiled tenderly. "No other woman exists for me, but you. When I hold you like this—" his hand swept over her "—touch you like this, I'm blind and deaf to everyone but you."

He took her then, filled her, drove her back into the storm. She followed the rhythm he set, dancing to the primitive song, moving in perfect counterpoint. The storm built, sliding into their veins and thundering through them. He rode the wild center of it, struggling for a control that escaped his grasp. What was happening between them defied control, defied anything and everything but absolute surrender.

It had been like that last time, too, so different from every other sexual experience that it had made an indelible impact on him. How could he have ever thought he'd made love to Alyssa all those weeks ago, when every touch, every sound, every movement and scent whispered Miri's name? No, not whispered. Shouted. Screamed. She'd branded him with her essence, made herself a permanent part of him. And he wanted to mark her the same way.

He surged into her, driving them together again and again in a frenzy of need. He threw back his head, wanting to howl at the moon, mindless with desire. It was no different for her. Her expression glowed in the silver light, more beautiful and wildly iridescent than he'd ever seen it.

And then the storm reached its height, broke over them, giving them up to ecstasy. They went over the edge together, united in heart, body and soul. She cried afterward, from joy, she tearfully insisted. Murmuring ridiculous words of reassurance, he lifted her in his arms and carried her back into the lake. There he gently washed the sand from her body. When he was through he took her to their improvised bed. Towels became blankets, cocooning them from the cool night breeze.

As sleep claimed them, he tucked her close and gave her his heart.

CHAPTER TEN

EARLY morning sunlight woke them. Miri stirred, so comfortable she didn't want to move, much less get up. She lay on her side, wrapped partially in towels and partially in Brandt, her head cushioned against his shoulder.

His gruff voice rumbled above her. "I'm thinking we should have hung up our clothes."

She laughed softly. "If it came down to a choice between that and what we did instead, I'll take option number two."

"I think I will, too."

"You think?" She poked him in the ribs, drawing a husky chuckle. "You better know, Your Highness."

"Oh, I know, all right."

Her amusement faded. "How do you suppose the fire started? Was it something I did?"

"Funny you should ask. I'd just been wondering if it was something I'd done wrong." His brows drew together. "I'm pretty sure we left one of the lamps burning in the main room. I was so angry when we went to bed, I didn't give it a thought. I'm guessing the wind must have blown the lamp over. Or maybe something flammable blew up against it."

"Frightening." She curled closer, lifting her head so she could watch his expression. "Brandt—"

"Uh-oh."

"We need to finish our discussion from last night." A wry note crept into her voice. "Though I wouldn't mind if we did it without losing our temper or starting any more fires."

He released his breath in a gusty sigh. "No promises, but we can give it a shot."

"Do you still insist we go our separate ways?" Determination filled her. "Fair warning, marriage or not, I plan to stand by you regardless of what happens with the allegations."

He tucked an arm behind his head and stared out at the lake. The fact that he avoided her gaze didn't bode well. "Once the allegations against me have been disproved so they can't adversely affect your reputation, you can do anything you want."

A tentative hope sparked to life. "Are you saying that after your name is cleared we can be together again?"

"That's just it, Miri. Nothing may happen." His expression turned brooding. "There may never be clarity. I may remain under suspicion forever, living beneath a shadow I can't escape."

She stared in disbelief. "Is that an admission of guilt? Because if it is, I'm not buying it. I know you, Brandt. You'd never steal from your own country."

"Someone wants it to look like I have," he argued doggedly. "The charges—"

"Will be cleared up, just like they were with Lander," Miri stated firmly. "Juliana's agreed to examine the records again. And don't you dare rant and rave at me about involving her. When it comes to finances and accounting there's no one better. You're lucky she's willing to help. Juliana will figure it out."

"And if she doesn't?" He turned to look at her then. At some point in the last day deep crevices had carved a path on either side of his mouth. A tightness gathered around his eyes—eyes flat with exhaustion. "It's not like she has a lot of incentive to clear me. As things stand now, your brother will win the election by a landslide. Why would she do anything to change that?"

"You're not the only honorable person in Verdonia, Brandt." Miri put a sting in the words. "You're not the only one who puts duty and responsibility ahead of personal desire or self-interest, or who has Verdonia's best interests at heart. Juliana is an honorable person. So are Lander and Merrick and Alyssa. The problem is you don't trust the Montgomerys. I'm not sure you even trust me."

He jackknifed upward, spilling towels in every direction. "What the hell are you talking about? Of course, I trust you."

"You don't trust me enough to let me in." She sat up, as well, fumbling to retrieve some of their covers. "I don't need your protection, Brandt. I don't need you to take care of me. I'm quite able to handle that job all on my own. What I want is a partner. A lover. A confidante. Isn't that what you want, too?"

A muscle jerked in his cheek. "Yes."

"But you still won't offer that, will you?"

"No."

She'd asked for frankness, and she'd certainly gotten it. She struggled to change tactics. In the little time they'd had together, she'd discovered that logic worked best with him. Granted, it wasn't her strong suit, but she'd give it a stab if it meant getting through to him. "You wouldn't be asking me to leave if our marriage hadn't been annulled," she pointed out. "Or if I'd actually been pregnant."

"I explained my reasoning on that."

"I remember. You would have been honor-bound to protect the baby. To give it your name." Curling her legs beneath her, she gathered up one of his hands and laced her fingers with his. "While you're so busy considering honor and duty, maybe you should consider one more important detail."

"Which is?"

"You abducted me and brought me back to Avernos. You announced to the world that I was your wife. You insisted I sleep in your bed. Basically, you compromised me. What effect do you suppose that will have on my reputation, and the manner in which people regard me? Whether or not I'm pregnant, your honor won't allow you to do anything other than marry me. And I can guarantee, my mother and brothers won't accept anything less, either."

"You...I—"

"We," she emphasized. "Not 'you' and not 'I,' but we. That's how it's supposed to be and how it's going to be from now on. You don't have to let me in, if you don't want. It's your choice. But every time you leave your home, you're going to find me camped on your doorstep. I'm hoping you'll eventually get tired of stepping over me and let me in."

"Damn it, Miri. I won't be stepping over anyone if I'm in prison."

"Brandt—"

"No more." He sat up, tossing aside towels, baring them. "Come on, Princess. Let's see if there's anything useful left out there."

She let the topic die. For now. It would give her time to regroup and come up with a new slew of arguments. "What about our clothes?" she asked, looking around for where they'd ended up. "I doubt they're dry."

"Then you'll have a choice. You can either wear wet, sticky clothes, or leave them off. Personally, I think you'll be more comfortable without them, though I'm not sure I'll be more comfortable watching you run around nude." He pretended to consider, a wicked gleam sparking to life in his black gaze. "I will, however, enjoy it more."

She scrambled up, wishing she was as relaxed and unabashed in her own skin as Brandt seemed to be. She considered his suggestion, to saying the hell with everything and embracing her wild side. The idea lasted an entire two seconds before she found herself scooping up one of the clean towels with a studied indifference and wrapping it around herself. It earned her a slow grin before Brandt followed suit.

While he headed toward the remains of the cabin, Miri tracked down their clothes. Sure enough, they were still wet and she spread them in the grass to dry, shaking her head over their condition.

Her nightgown was a disaster. Aside from several small rents in the skirt and in the seams, it also had numerous burn holes from the hot ash, and the soot-stained hem was ripped loose. Brandt's clothes had fared little better, probably as a result of his race through the woods to reach her. Both shirt and trousers were torn, some showing bloodstains where branches or vines had snagged more than cloth. He'd also collected his fair share of burn holes and soot marks, as well.

Realizing she couldn't do anything more about their clothes, she joined Brandt. She found him waiting for her not far from the cabin. The fire had finally died, all that remained a pile of glowing embers. She shivered at the grim sight. Luck had been with them last night, tragedy barely averted. As though picking up on her distress, he slung an arm around her shoulders and held her close.

"Come on. This is pointless," he said. "Let's check out the boathouse and see what we can find there."

"Fishing poles would be nice." Her stomach

grumbled. "A fresh trout breakfast would be even better."

"I'll see what I can do."

They did have their trout breakfast, though it took a few more hours than Miri would have liked. Even so, it was well worth the wait. By the time they'd eaten, their clothes were dry enough to wear, though she felt ridiculous running around in a nightgown. Still, it was better than a towel. Barely.

Standing by the boathouse while they returned the fishing poles to their proper places, Miri stared out across the lake and frowned. "Why does this place seem so familiar to me?" she muttered. Brandt had started to tell her yesterday when the helicopter's departure had interrupted them. She swung around to ask again. "Tell me about the time I was last here."

He regarded her in surprise. "You really don't remember? I thought that was just a ploy to distract me."

"Well, yes." She fought back a blush. "But it

was a sincere question. I really have been here before?"

"You and your family came to the palace to celebrate my grandfather's seventy-fifth birthday. The next morning we all drove out here to spend the day at the lake."

She shook her head. "I don't remember."

"You should. It was the first time I rescued you."

"That was here?" She stared at the lake and surrounding woods with new eyes, trying to equate memory with reality. "I guess it was such a traumatic experience, I put it out of my head. I remember begging my brothers to play hide-and-seek. And then…" Her brow crinkled in a frown. "I got lost and you found me. Is that what happened?" she asked uncertainly.

"You found a small cavern and squeezed inside. Then you couldn't get out again. It took hours to find you."

"You were the one who got me out." Wonder lit her eyes. "How could I have forgotten? You sat there and talked to me for the longest time until I'd calmed down. That's when I first fell in love with you. You told me to feel around for a pebble and hold it in my hand because it was magical and could shrink me small enough to squeeze back out. And it worked. Or at least, I believed it did at the time. I still have it in my jewelry box. It's the prettiest stone—" She broke off with a gasp.

"What is it? What's wrong?" His head jerked skyward. "Got it. I hear it, too. The helicopter's returning."

"No, that's not what I meant. Brandt—"

He caught her hand. "Come on. Rescue party's here."

"Wait. Brandt, wait! You have to listen to me."

The helicopter dipped low, making a curving sweep along the lakeshore, the noise from its propellers drowning out her voice. It landed in the exact same spot as yesterday. Within seconds of touching down, Tolken emerged from the still churning copter, appearing distinctly white-faced.

He sketched a deep, humble bow. "I apologize, Your Highness, for my part in yesterday's events, as well as for not getting here sooner. Less than an hour ago we received reports from a pair of hikers of a possible fire. Are you and Princess Miri hurt? Do you require medical attention?"

"That won't be necessary. We could use a change of clothes, but we're fine otherwise."

Tolken's gaze flickered in Miri's direction and then swiftly away. "I have a spare jumpsuit stashed in the helicopter. It'll be a trifle large for Her Highness, but might be preferable to the alternative."

"Since the alternative is my nightgown, I'm forced to agree," Miri inserted dryly. "If you'll get it for me, I'll change in the boathouse."

"Yes, Your Highness."

The instant he returned to the helicopter, Miri

grabbed Brandt's arm. "Before we go, I need to speak to you in private. It's important."

He shook his head. "Enough, Miri. There's nothing left to be said. We both have our own opinions about honor and duty, and I don't see either of us changing our mind anytime soon."

"It's not about that. It's—"

Tolken hustled back, a bright orange pair of coveralls in his hands. Left with no choice, Miri snatched it up and headed for the boathouse to change. The outfit was huge, leaving her swimming in an ocean of orange. Acres of excess material dangled off her wrists and ankles, tripping her every time she tried to take a step. Opening the door, she called for Brandt.

"Hey, I need help in here."

He broke off his conversation with Tolken. Not that it was much of a conversation. It looked more like he was giving the poor man hell. With a final hard comment, he left a visibly shaken Tolken and approached, his stride long and lethal, reminding her more than ever of a stalking panther. Heaven help her, His Highness was back in charge and didn't appear to be in the best of tempers. So much for last night. So much for the gentle man who'd held her through the night. Comforted her. Made love to her.

He entered the boathouse and pushed the door to behind him. "What's the problem, Miri? We need to leave."

"And you need to listen." Before he could interrupt again, she flipped her dangling cuff at him. "First, help me with this stupid thing. It's dragging every which way."

"Then we leave. No more talking."

Together they rolled up the material at her wrists and ankles. She looked down at herself with a sigh. "I look ridiculous, don't I?"

He nodded. "Just a bit."

"Gee, thanks," she grumbled. "You're supposed to say I look adorable."

"Your nightgown looked adorable. This…not so much."

"That bad?" She grabbed a pair of rubber sandals from off one of the storage racks and slipped them on. "Bad enough to keep you from ravishing me?"

He waited a beat. "Never that bad."

"Okay, then. I feel better now." When he would have opened the door again, she caught hold of his hand. "Listen, Brandt. That cavern. The one where you found me all those years ago? Do you think you can find it again?"

"I'm not sure. Maybe." He frowned impatiently. "You don't mean today?"

"Yes, today," she insisted. "As in, right now, this minute."

He shook his head before she'd even finished speaking. "That's impossible. According to Tolken, there's a situation brewing back at the palace. I'm needed there."

She waved that aside, nearly unraveling her sleeve again. "Forget the palace. This can't wait." She didn't want to tell him of her suspicions, not if it meant raising his hopes, only to dash then again. Not when it promised to cement his determination to get rid of her. But she could see he was going to refuse her request and desperation had her speaking without consideration. "I'll make you a deal. If you'll do as I ask, I'll agree to return to my family without a fight." Oh, God, what was she saying? "I'll… I'll do whatever you want about our future, no matter how thickheaded and foolish I consider it."

Okay, maybe that last part could have been phrased better, considering she hoped to win his cooperation. But really. He was being thickheaded and foolish by refusing to allow her to stand at his side while he faced the charges being leveled against him.

She could tell her impulsive offer had given him pause and he studied her in the dim light seeping into the boathouse. "You? A walking, talking argument? You'll do whatever I want?" His eyes narrowed. "What's going on, Miri?"

If she'd been a child, she'd have been jumping up and down and pleading incoherently by now. "I'll explain if you find the cavern. I might be wrong and I'd rather not say anything until I know for certain."

He shook his head. "It's been a long time and I'm not sure I remember exactly where it was."

"Please, Brandt. You have to try."

"And if I agree? Do we have a deal?" He spoke with his grandfather's voice, serious and regal. The voice of a man who ruled a principality, and one day, maybe, a country. "You'll return to your family as soon as we get back to the palace?"

She flinched from the ultimatum, but she'd made a promise and she'd stick to it. "Yes. We have a deal." She closed her eyes in despair. So, this was what sacrifice tasted like. She couldn't say she cared much for the flavor of it. The dish held far too bitter a bite. "I'll return to my family as soon as we get back to the palace."

He jerked his head toward the door. "Come on, then. Let's go."

"Wait."

He thrust a hand through his hair. "What now, Miri?"

"Before we go…" She moistened her lips. "I want you to kiss me one last time."

He stilled. "Is this some sort of trick?"

She laughed, hoping against hope he couldn't hear the underlying tears. "No trick. Just a goodbye kiss, that's all I'm asking."

He didn't argue further. Hooking his index finger into the plunging neckline of her coveralls, he propelled her into his arms. And then he kissed her, driving every thought from her mind but the need to lose herself in his embrace. He took her mouth with exquisite tenderness and she moaned softly, opening to him. His tongue mated with hers, teasing her toward the raw, primal urges she'd experienced both times he'd made love to her. It only took that one kiss for her to want again, to be filled with a fierce longing to have him take her the way he had last night. One touch, and she lost all rational thought.

His reaction was no different. Sunlight streamed through the narrow gap in the door and fell directly on his face. Harsh color slashed across his cheekbones, the wildfire burning in his eyes glittering with deadly intent. He was a man reduced to his most primitive, his desire raw and blatant. She stared up at him. Breath and heartbeat quickened. If the time and place had been any different, he'd have taken their embrace to its ultimate conclusion.

But it wasn't another time or place, and she'd made a deal. Snatching a final kiss, whispering a silent farewell, she released him and stepped back. "Thank you, Your Highness," she managed to say. Crossing to the door, she flung it open and stepped into the painfully bright sunshine. If she blinked hard, it was only because her eyes were slow to adjust to the light. Nothing more, most certainly not tears.

Turning to Brandt, she gestured toward the surrounding wood. "Which way?"

The search proved hot and exhausting. More than once Miri was on the verge of giving up. But there was too much at stake to quit. "Try again," she urged when they hit another false trail.

"I know you couldn't have gotten too far from the lake. The brush has probably grown up around the cavern," Brandt said, wiping the sweat from his brow. He paused to study the surrounding terrain. "It should be on a hillside."

She pointed farther out. "We haven't checked there."

He hesitated, before nodding. "I would have thought that's too far, but it took a while to find you when you originally went missing. So, let's give it a try."

As soon as they approached the area, he picked up his pace. "This is it. I'm sure it's over here."

And there it was, a narrow slash in the earth. Miri could only stare at it, shaking her head. How in the world had she managed to fit in there, even at the tender age of eleven? She approached the cavern and dropped to her knees, grateful for the bulky coveralls. Carefully, she slid her arm into the opening and groped along the floor, gathering up a handful of the pebbles. Sending up a silent prayer, she pulled her arm from the opening and slowly opened her hand. Sunlight struck the stones she held.

"Are these what I think they are?" she asked Brandt unevenly.

Crouching beside her, he expelled his breath in a long sigh. "Only if you think they're Juliana Rose amethysts."

CHAPTER ELEVEN

"How did you know?" Brandt asked, shaking his head in amazement.

She examined the stones with a practiced eye. "It was Juliana's wedding ring that tipped me off. That new colored amethyst looked so familiar for some reason. I couldn't think why until you reminded me about getting trapped in the cavern when I was eleven. Then it clicked. I remembered the pebble I'd kept from that day and the odd color and—" She threw herself into his arms. "Oh, Brandt. I can't believe we found more of them. Wait until everyone finds out that those few in her ring aren't the only Juliana Roses in existence."

He gathered her into a tight embrace, resting his cheek against the top of her head. How many more times would he be able to hold her like this before he'd be forced to let her go? "Honey, we need to keep this a secret until we're certain about what we have here."

"Yes, of course. I won't say a word." A small frown touched her brow. "How soon can you get a geologist to the site?"

"I'll have a crew out here before the end of the day."

"That soon?" She beamed in delight. "And how long before they know how large the deposit is? Tomorrow? The end of the week?"

"Slow down, Miri," he cautioned. "It could be a while. Accuracy is more important than speed."

"But if it's a large deposit?" The hope filling her eyes was painful to watch. "Will it be enough?"

"It could save Verdonia." He held up a hand to stem her excited exclamation. "Let's not get too worked up. We have to wait for the initial report to come in. And then for the final one. A lot can happen between now and then."

"In the meantime, maybe Juliana has discovered something about the accusations against you." It was her turn to cut him off. "Don't tell me not to get my hopes up. I'm not all doom and gloom like you. I want to believe that everything will work out. I've already decided that my darling sister-in-law will clear you and our find is going to be the tip of a huge mine full of Juliana Rose amethysts. Don't bother trying to talk me out of it. That's what's going to happen. My mind is made up."

He couldn't help but smile. Miri's green eyes glowed with excitement, her cheeks as bright a pink as her lips. Dirt smudged the side of her nose and her hair remained in a hopeless tangle down her back. But he'd never seen her look more beautiful. Unable to resist, he snatched a kiss. The color in both cheek and lip deepened.

Reluctantly letting her go, he hunkered down in front of the slash and scooped up another handful of stones, dropping them into his pocket. From what little he could tell without the appropriate equipment, they showed serious promise for depth of color, size and clarity. He'd be very interested to hear what his master cutter had to say about them.

Looking around for a suitable rock, he gestured to Miri. "Unroll one of your sleeves. I want to mark this spot." He used the sharp edge from a piece of quartz to jab a hole in the material. Ripping it, he tore free a strip of orange and tied it to a nearby bush. "Okay, let's go. We've done everything we can here. I need to take care of whatever crisis is going down at the palace."

She threw the cavern a final excited glance before falling in beside him on their return trek through the woods. Tolken and the pilot were waiting patiently by the helicopter, ready to lift off at a moment's notice. The ride back to the palace took no time, and no sooner did they step from the craft than one of his guards came for them at a dead run.

He sketched a hasty bow. "Please, Your Highness. All hell's breaking loose in there—" He gulped when he realized what he'd said, and stared at Miri in horror. "Begging your pardon, ma'am."

She waved aside the apology. "What's going on? What's happening?"

"I think they've come to arrest Prince Brandt. They're all in there arguing." He turned back to Brandt. "If you would, Your Highness. You need to come."

"Go tell them I'm on my way."

He would have followed the guard if Miri hadn't thrown herself in front of him. "No. No, you're not going."

"Sweetheart—"

"Don't sweetheart me." She gripped his shirt and one of the seams gave way. "You listen to me. I don't want to hear another word about duty, or honor or responsibility. And so help me, if the word sacrifice ever leaves your mouth again, I swear, I won't be held accountable for my actions."

"I am who I am," he stated simply.

Her chin wobbled. "And I love who you are, Brandt. Even those truly annoying parts."

He offered a slow smile. "Thanks."

"If you go in there, I'm going with you. And I'm going as your wife."

He shook his head. "You aren't my wife."

"I will be," she said fiercely. "I don't care if I have to tie you up and drag you in front of the nearest church official, we will be married. You will allow me to stand by your side while you face these charges."

His smile faded. "You made a bargain with me, or have you forgotten?" From the way her face went stark white, he realized she had. "You promised to return to your family and I intend to hold you to your word."

"Don't. Please don't make me leave you."

She was killing him, slicing off pieces of his soul. "When my name is cleared—"

"No! Not when it's cleared. Right now, when it counts most. I want to declare my love openly. I want the entire world to know how I feel about you." Tears choked her. "Please, Brandt. I know you can't say the words back. Honor won't allow you to. But I want you to hear them from me. Here. Now."

Her hands crept to his face, smoothing each harsh line with a tender caress. He'd never seen such blatant adoration on a person's face before. The fact that it was for him was humbling.

"I love you," she said. "I love you more than I ever thought possible. I'll love you until the day I die. And then somehow, someway, I'll love you for all of eternity. When we go in there and face whatever there is to face, if you'll let me, I intend to shout my feelings to the entire world. But for right now, in this instant of time, my feelings are private and for you alone."

He enfolded her in his arms, knowing it was

the last time he'd ever hold her. Cupping her face, he brushed away her tears. "If I were a free man, if I were any man but the one I am, I would tell you I love you, too. But I can't as long as I'm under suspicion. I can't tell you that I adore you, that you are my life. I can't tell you that you're more precious to me than all the amethysts in Verdonia. I can't tell you that more than anything I want our night together to have borne fruit, to watch you ripen with my child. I can't tell you how much I long to spend the rest of my life making you happy." He kissed her, a lingering kiss of farewell. "If it weren't wrong, I'd tell you that I'll love you today, tomorrow and every tomorrow until the end of time."

The guard had reappeared, almost dancing with impatience, and Brandt reluctantly released her. "I have to go, sweetheart."

"At least let me stand by you through this much," she pleaded.

"Your Highness?" the guard interrupted. "I

thought I should let you know that Princess Miri's family is in the study with everyone else. They've requested her presence, as well."

Her surprise gave way to sheer delight. "Perfect. You were going to send me back to my family. Now we both get what we want." She glanced down at herself and gave a small gasp of horror. "We are not facing them like this. I'm sure everyone can wait five minutes while we clean up."

By the time they'd showered and changed, it was closer to thirty minutes than five. They headed for his study hand in hand. Miri wore her red power suit and mile-high heels, no doubt for courage, and she'd coiled her hair in a sophisticated knot that made her appear every inch the princess.

"Did you have to wear black?" she asked him in a disapproving undertone. "It makes you look like you're going to your funeral."

"Entirely possible." He paused outside his study, stopping her heated response with a shake of his head. "I don't know what we're going to find when we go in there, but no matter how it goes down, I don't want you to interfere."

Her mouth compressed at the order, but she nodded, worry deepening the color of her eyes. "I'll try not to say anything."

Honest, if not quite what he'd asked. Still, it would have to do. Strident voices came from behind the heavy wooden door. Many voices, both male and female. Turning the knob, he pushed open the door. Inside, he found sheer pandemonium.

At first, all he could see were Montgomerys, every last one of the royals, as far as he could tell. Even Joc Arnaud, Juliana's brother, was present, lending weight to the proceedings. They surrounded the chair in front of his desk where a small cringing man sat, clutching a briefcase to his chest as though it were a lifeline. The chief executive councilman of the TGC, if he didn't miss his guess. And they were all shouting at him, even Miri's mother, Rachel. Off to one side hovered Alyssa's mother, Angela. And holding her in an embrace that looked as intimate as it did comforting stood Erik Sutherland.

"Interesting. I thought Erik was Angela's stepson," he said sotto voce. "That hug doesn't look terribly maternal."

Miri gave a soft laugh. "Boy, are you out of date. I was just a baby at the time, but maybe you have a vague memory of Erik's father divorcing Angela?"

"A very vague memory. Alyssa was…what? A year, maybe two at the time? That would have put Erik in his early twenties."

"That's about right. Well, the reason for Angela's divorce from Prince Frederick is hugging her as we speak."

"So, Alyssa…"

"Is Erik's daughter, not Prince Frederick's." Miri's eyes narrowed in speculation. "What I'd like to know is why the two of them are here. What do they have to do with all this?"

"I'm almost afraid to ask. But I can't help wondering if it has something to do with Erik abdicating to Alyssa. If he hadn't, she wouldn't be ruling Celestia right now."

"And you wouldn't have tried to marry her in order to win the election."

He winced at the tart edge to Miri's tongue. "Bygones, love. Water definitely under the bridge." He scrutinized the group around the councilman. "Hell. I'm not sure I want to wade into the middle of that mess."

As though his comment caught everyone's attention, all focus honed in on them. They were instantly enveloped in Montgomerys, every last one of them talking at once. Brandt folded his arms across his chest and waited it out. As soon as it became clear they weren't planning to stop anytime soon, he held up a hand. To his surprise, they actually fell silent.

"What the hell is going on?" he asked mildly.

The councilman hastened to his feet and offered a small, awkward bow that left him juggling with his briefcase. "I apologize, Your Highness. But I've come to inform you a warrant has been sworn out for your arrest."

Lander turned to confront the man. "And we're telling you, you're not arresting him. My wife has evidence—"

"That the documents you have are forgeries," Juliana broke in, waving a sheathe of papers. "And I can prove it."

The councilman bobbed his head. "Yes, Your Highness. I understand your position. But we've voted and—"

"You're going to have to take another vote," Merrick spoke up. "Because my security force has no intention of allowing you to arrest von Folke and that's the end of it."

"Please, Your Highness. Your Highnesses," the councilman pleaded. "You can't do this. The TGC has proof of these improprieties. Now, I understand you have conflicting evidence, but until this is straightened out, I have no choice. I have my orders. Lauren DeVida had help stealing the amethysts and getting them out of the country. All the evidence points to Prince Brandt. He has control of the mines and is in charge of transporting the gemstones from those mines to Celestia. He must be stopped before we lose any more amethysts. The discrepancies we've uncovered point to his being responsible for some very serious…er… accounting errors."

"Accounting errors or thefts?" Brandt asked in a deadly voice.

"Thefts," the councilman squeaked.

"Erik," Angela urged. "You have to tell them the truth. Explain about Lauren and why you abdicated."

Erik nodded, squaring his shoulders. "Lauren DeVida did have help. But it was my father, Prince Frederick, who helped her. After his death, I found documents implicating him. I…I chose to abdicate because of it." His voice faltered. "It seemed the only honorable course of action. To try and make amends, I did my best to track the woman down and have her brought to justice."

"Did you find her?" Brandt asked, genuinely curious.

"Two days ago. She's in custody and being extradited to Verdonia. She's agreed to cooperate fully with the investigation. We won't recover all the money, but we'll get a large portion of it back."

Everyone started talking at once. Brandt bowed his head, struggling to take it all in. "They supported you," Miri said in a soft voice. "They defended you. All of them."

"I...I didn't expect that." Unable to resist, he pulled her close. "You were right about them, sweetheart. They are honorable. All of them."

"Do you finally believe your name—*our* name—will be cleared now?"

He laughed, the sound a tad rusty, but still a laugh. "I believe."

"Then do I have your permission to say something now?" The demure question was contradicted by the mischievous gleam in her eyes.

He swept her an elegant bow. "Now that my name is cleared, I release you from your bargain. You're free to say anything you wish."

"In that case…" She raised her voice. "Will you marry me?"

That silenced the entire room. Brandt released his breath in an exaggerated sigh. "Considering how badly you've compromised me, I don't see that I have any choice. Yes, I'll marry you. For real, this time."

And then pandemonium broke loose again.

The sun broke across the mountains on Miri's wedding day, pouring its warmth and light across Avernos like a loving balm. The palace overflowed with guests from every corner of Verdonia, all of whom found cause to dart into Miri's room for a quick visit before the ceremony. Not that she minded. As far as she was concerned, sharing her happiness added to her enjoyment of the festivities.

Finally, it came time to dress and everyone left except her mother, and Juliana and Alyssa, who helped Miri get ready. The wedding gown she'd ultimately chosen was as different from that first ceremony as she could have wished. Dainty, elegant, romantic, it was the sort of gown she'd always hoped to wear when she married. In celebration of the discovery of the largest supply of Juliana Rose and Royal amethysts in Verdonia's history, the bodice was liberally studded with both gemstones, as was her veil. They were a statement, each glittering flash a promise to Verdonia of future harmony and prosperity.

A few hours later, standing in the vestibule of the chapel moments before the wedding was scheduled to begin, she couldn't help but compare the two ceremonies she'd experienced here. Only there was no comparison. One had been darkness and despair. This was light and joy. One had been the result of bitterness and the need for vengeance. This was a marriage of love, the bonding of heart, mind and soul.

There was no thunderous processional to escort her up the aisle this time, only the soft strains of a string quartet. Instead of walking the endless length on her own, she clung to Lander's arm. He'd honored the occasion by dressing in full military uniform, right down to white gloves and a saber strapped to his side. When they reached the altar, Lander joined her hand with Brandt's. Then he crossed to the front pew where the entire Montgomery family stood in beaming approval and joined his wife, Juliana, and her brother, financial wizard, Joc Arnaud.

Through the layers of lace and tulle, she saw Brandt give her a slow, teasing smile. Snagging the hem of her veil he lifted it and peeked beneath. "Just checking," he explained to their guests.

Laughter rippled through the chapel. Where before the ceremony had been torturous, cold and deliberate, this time a warmth and lightness permeated. Most poignant of all were the vows, spoken with such love and sincerity, there was no doubting that the wedding was a love match.

Once again they were pronounced husband and wife, and this time Brandt not only lifted her veil, but swept it completely off her head, releasing her hair from its elegant coil. It streamed down her shoulders and back and he thrust his fingers deep into the loosened strands. "I love you," he told his wife. "You are more important than anything else in my life."

And then he kissed her, a kiss of promise. Of honor and duty and responsibility. There was only one thing missing in the kiss he gave her. Sacrifice. Instead of sacrifice, they found healing. When he finally released her there wasn't a dry eye in the chapel.

Turning, they started to make their way back down the aisle, when Lander stepped from his pew, directly into their path. For a long minute the two men faced each other, two men who would be king. The tension grew, stretching nerves to the limit. Then Lander did something that shocked Miri to the core. In a smooth, practiced move, he unsheathed his saber from its scabbard and offered it to Brandt. Utter silence descended on the chapel.

Brandt hesitated. "Are you certain?" he asked in a voice only the three of them could hear.

"It's time for a change. Verdonia needs you."

"It needs you and Merrick, as well." There was no doubting Brandt's sincerity. "I would appreciate your help."

"You'll have it."

With a nod of agreement, Brandt accepted the sword. He signaled to the musicians, who immediately resumed playing the recessional. Then he and Miri continued their trip down the aisle. Instead of waiting in the vestibule to greet their guests, he ushered her outside. Brilliant sunshine greeted them. Urging her onward, they cut through the courtyard and into the garden. Crossing to the far end, he set the saber on a bench adjacent to the woods.

Miri stared at it. "When Lander gave you his sword…did that mean what I think it did?"

"It was a gesture of fealty," Brandt confirmed. "By tomorrow the news will be all over Verdonia." He shook his head in disbelief. "He just handed me the election."

Tears filled her eyes. "I told you he was an honorable man."

"With all that's happened, Verdonia needs him more than ever. As do I. He won't regret what he's done today."

It was then that she recognized the significance of where they were standing. "Do you realize that this is where it all started?" She gestured toward the bench. "That's where I took Alyssa's place."

Brandt folded his arms across his chest. "We've come full circle."

"The perfect 'happily ever after' moment?" she asked in an odd voice.

He smiled, that slow, sweet smile of his. "Can you think of a better one?"

"Just one." She returned to his arms. "Remember our night at the cabin? The night of the fire?"

His breath escaped in a laugh. "How could I forget? It's indelibly printed on my memory for so many reasons. But mainly..." He took her mouth in a leisurely kiss, one of barely restrained passion. One that hinted of what they'd share when the day was through. "Mainly I remember because of what came after the fire."

"Something else came of that night. Something very special and unexpected." She caught his hand in hers and cupped it low on her abdomen. "There's someone here, my love. Someone who wants to say hello to you."

* * * * *